GRAVE REVELATIONS

BOOK TWO OF THE INFINITE CYCLE

by Kenneth W. Cain

"This is a special sword." Yu held it in both hands, offering it to Marty.

Marty didn't think now the right time to take the sword. He would need to earn this privilege.

A wrinkle furled on Yu's forehead. "What are you doing?"

"Looking at the sword."

"Well, why aren't you picking it up?" Even with the accent, Yu's English was good.

Marty's cheeks flushed, and he took the sword. He supposed the time for formalities had passed with the hives. Yu wanted him to get a good look at the sword, and Marty couldn't help but chuckle as he observed it, having derived the notion from watching too many late-night movies. The sword was lighter than he expected, and shorter. He took the black leather-bound handle in his palm and wrapped his fingers around it. The sword felt comfortable in his hand, as if it belonged there. He studied the delicate red ribbon wrapped around the scabbard. Light purple letters lined the ribbon, spelling out a message in a language Marty couldn't read.

Yu wore an amused grin. He demonstrated how to withdraw the sword from its scabbard. Marty watched, then repeated the action, not all the way but far enough to see the etching on one side of the blade.

"What does this mean?" Marty asked.

Yu looked at the etching, though Marty suspected he didn't need to. It was probable he had memorized the words, yet, still Yu's eyes thinned on the markings, as if trying to read them. His dark hair wavered in a light breeze as he gazed out across the decimated cityscape. "Not yet, my friend." He sounded distant, as if lost in his memories. He turned back to Marty. "That is a lesson for another day. First, we learn patience and precision. We honor our sword."

For Laura

Chapter 1

Over the edge of the mountain, a storm approached, the crystal blue sky isolating it. Dave watched with interest.

What is that? A rogue tornado?

They were rare in these parts of Pennsylvania, but that didn't mean it was impossible. The dark formation ebbed toward his farm, as if his homestead were some magnetic force attracting it. Unsure of whether to run for shelter or stand his ground, Dave contemplated what action to take as the formation of blackened clouds inched closer to his location.

"Dave? What is it?"

He turned to his wife, Carol, standing in the doorway. She had been his partner in life for fifty-two years. In this morning light, she couldn't have looked more beautiful. His one true love, he was thankful to have her company, even with what few flaws she had.

"I'm not sure."

He returned his attention to the storm, surprised how close it loomed now after just a few minutes. Dark tendrils swirled within the clouds, raising new concerns for Dave. Unsettling worry consumed him, having never witnessed such a thing in all his years. It was for that reason he didn't go running for shelter.

"I think we should dig in, honey." Carol waved him inward.

He looked back at her, still unsure of how to respond. The thought to tell her to go, to leave him here, crossed his mind. The words to express that thought though had yet to find his mouth. Instead, he only stared at her, bemused by the way her silver hair teased in the storm winds—

If that's even what it is…

Then the dark formation was upon them, and it was too late to run and hide anywhere. Both Carol and he were in the direct path, about to come face to face with whatever wrath it would deliver. The shock of what he was seeing dumbfounded him.

A single bright ray of light burst from the clouds, striking the ground in a perfect circle, about the size of a car. Seeing this left Dave uncertain upon, seeing the area of ground it enlightened. It was Carol who broke the silence.

"Jesus Christ!" She shielded her eyes with one hand and held her dress tight against her body with the other.

Dave followed her eyes, expecting to see something terrifying. Instead, within the beam of light, a naked man descended upon them. Dave's jaw fell open in disbelief.

"It's Jesus Christ, Dave," Carol clarified. She appeared to have regained some spring in her knees, as she started bouncing around about with glee. "He's come to take us home, baby." Her eyes welled with tears of joy. "Our savior has come back for us." She rocked to the rhythm of some unheard hymn she sang in her head.

Dave wanted to tell her what a silly notion that was—he had never taken to what she called *The Word of God*. An honest man with humble beliefs, seeing this phenomenon made it hard to deny anything, no matter how strange it sounded.

When the otherworldly man touched down, Carol sprang forward and dropped to his feet in a bowing gesture. She crawled closer to him on her knees, making sure not to cross into the area of light, as if this action would be blasphemous. Dave suspected she thought herself unworthy of the light because they hadn't been the church-going sort in a long time.

She peered up at the man, regarding him with gentle, caring eyes. "Oh Lord," she cried out. "Take us. We will obey you, dear Lord."

Dave couldn't relent himself so willfully. He eyed the man, noting his near perfect golden-brown hair. Looking past the well-groomed facial hair, the man's eyes were unlike any color he had seen before, appearing as glowing orange pools of light.

Dave spoke the only words he could find at the moment. "Son, you know your butt ass naked, don't you?"

"Dave!" Carol shook a scolding finger at her husband, as if to remind him of his place. "You don't point out those types of things to the Lord Jesus Christ."

An urge to correct Carol lingered on his tongue, as nothing had proven this stranger was the Lord to him. No miracles had occurred—unless you considered a man had just descended from the sky in a beam of light one. Dave considered this, as it wasn't an everyday occurrence. Furthering his doubt, the beam of light faded and the clouds above the man eroded into the afternoon sky. There had been no storm after all—only this man. It was the nature of his arrival that left Dave unsettled.

"Do we know you, son?" Dave said.

The man regarded him for the first time, taking a bold step closer to Dave, ignoring the scampering Carol on the grassy earth at his feet. As the man passed her, Dave was certain he had seen her kiss the stranger's feet. Thankfully, they looked clean, and absent of any visible sores.

Standing before Dave, the man regarded his stature. His orange-hued eyes traced Dave's frame up and down before moving to his wife. The man studied her as well before returning to Dave.

Sadness fell over the stranger. "You are not my brother."

Dave considered this more of a question than a statement, one he wasn't sure how to respond to. "Son, I'm not sure—"

"We believe, my Lord," Carol cried out, still caught up in the passionate throws of religion.

The man ignored Carol's fanaticism, remaining focused on Dave. "I must find my brother, for I have come back for him."

"Who is your brother?" Dave asked.

The man came closer, his face mere inches from Dave's. The stranger's eyes seemed to pry inside of Dave's thoughts, attempting to draw out some bit of knowledge Dave didn't have. A supernatural swelling seized Dave's head, an inhuman sensation. Maybe this was a miracle. Dave was no longer sure of anything.

"Marty," the man said. "I need to find Marty."

Chapter 2

Fuck this, Ike thought. Fuck the onions. Fuck the peppers. And fuck those whosiewasits Becca likes, too.

Ike had tried to remain patient, but farming was hard for him, even if it was the way of things in this new world. Never had he been the sort to take to agriculture, anyway.

Hell, it's better than the alternative.

What if he was still all alone? No job, no partner, nothing. And with Becca wanting a child more and more lately, he had better figure out how to cultivate this land sooner rather than later.

He wondered when the electricity would come back on. Gazing across the valley, he doubted it would take long to return to normalcy once the government folk finally came out of hiding. They would know how to get matters back in order. But there was a looming doubt that things ever could be as they once were, before the aliens lay waste to most of the known world.

Most of what he heard had been rumors, as there was no television or radio anymore. Mostly, that news came as word of mouth, passed on from one passerby to another. Some claimed the Midwest was the only area affected. Others said hives had littered the landscape prior to the aliens collecting them into their ships. Some people fought back to the bitter end—Ike's group included—while the aliens took others prisoner with no form of aggression. If true, Ike wished all those backstabbing bastards would die off fast. He had fought and sacrificed—although if anyone asked him, he could not put any clear definition to how it applied to his specific case.

Truth told, Ike didn't know the truth anymore. He hadn't come across a single unaffected zone from Illinois to right inside the border of Pennsylvania. Everything along the way to his new home lay in waste, likely coming at the hands of mankind's own weaponry more so than the aliens. It was evidence they hadn't been able to contain the situation like they hoped.

What Ike knew was that the ones who sacrificed the most were Bernard and Marty. Or maybe, Marty and Nancy. Ike didn't care for the outcome—he'd rather be somewhere cool, drinking a good whisky—but, if living like this meant no more aliens, so be it.

Day after day, he waited, knowing at any moment those upside-down-faced bastards might return for another round. He had lost touch with the others, though he wasn't too far away to go see them if he wanted to. In part, he was thankful for the separation. He would be lying if he said the way both Bernard and Sheila stared up at the stars all the time didn't make him nervous. At first, it hadn't bothered him, but once he found Becca, everything changed. No longer could he think of himself. He had to think of her, and maybe a kid someday, too.

He stuck around those parts for a while, trying to help the others get accustomed to life without electricity. Once Becca started thinking about kids, though, he decided it best to settle down elsewhere, far away from any danger. Although he sometimes missed them, he hoped he would never see them again. Because of what seeing them again might mean.

Reaching the corn, Ike inspected his crop. All the ears were half the size they should be.

Crap!

Midget corn wouldn't impress Becca much. He still had a lot left to learn about farming. They were lucky he could grow out anything to eat at all. He supposed if she hadn't complained about his deformed carrots, she wouldn't find the corn too offensive, either. Sometimes he wished he had paid better attention to what Marty tried to teach him. But Ike always knew he wouldn't amount to much of a failed farmer. Farming was like a young boy getting laid for the first time to him—all thumbs, and always too early.

Gazing out across the horizon again, he wondered how his friends were doing. Almost a year had passed, and way too fast.

It occurred to him, *Even if they got the electricity back on, it would be a long while before I found out.*

Few knew his little stretch in Pennsylvania. That was in large why he fancied the place, its isolation from everyone. There weren't many neighbors to come around bugging him all the time. Determined to keep himself from ever ending up trapped within a crawl space ever again, he had found freedom here.

"Ike?" Becca leaned out the door. "Dinner."

He nodded, too caught up in memories to do much of anything else. Often, he wondered what became of Sandy. Not because of some childish crush, but he had a genuine concern over the fact they hadn't been able to find her after the dust settled. If she had ever offered, it would have been hard to turn down a piece of ass like that. But now he had to think of the bigger picture. He couldn't go around being a dick all the time, even if it came easier to him than it did most. There were too many responsibilities to consider, Becca being the foremost.

Maybe so, but you're no more a father than you are a farmer.

Becca went back inside.

Ike stayed a little longer, suddenly seeing a stranger approaching in the distance. The man's long hair flowed in the wind. His step was confident, as if walking with a sense of pride. Ike stayed his ground, gripping the hoe tighter, preparing for a confrontation. Then, as the grey-haired man came into view, he wondered why he hadn't recognized him sooner.

"Marty? What the fuck are you doing here?"

Extending his arms to receive his friend, Marty laughed. Ike hated to admit it, but it was good to see the old fart again—despite the underlying implications such a meeting suggested.

Marty blew a sharp-toned whistle through his pursed lips, directing it over his shoulder at some unseen thing. "Come, Bento."

Ike watched the dog scurry up beside his master, a Labrador.

Chapter 3

To Nancy, there was an eerie overtone to the manner in which Bernard left for work. She saw something in him she hadn't in a long while, though she couldn't quite place it. Was he walking a little straighter, as if his age hadn't already caught up to him? That could be. He had in fact been acting rather strange these last few days. Today, though, had been the worst by far.

Their small town was a place where give and take made their rebuilt world function. They didn't live too far away from Marty and Sheila, or even from Ike, but the farm life itself wasn't for them. They required some semblance of a city, and this was about as close to it as they had come, given the circumstances.

No need arose for a sheriff, not yet at least. People behaved, perhaps still traumatized by what they had only recently endured. There hadn't been too many stragglers passing through, either. Nancy knew as soon as the wrong people realized that, they could bully their way to anything they desired. It was the human condition. This would be when the looting and pillaging began. For now, though, peace prevailed.

She tried not to worry about such things. Others had it far worse than they did. Without television or consistent radio broadcasts, they had to rely on word of mouth. She had once heard a rumor the aliens wiped most of Mexico off the face of the Earth. If true, those people had suffered plenty beyond what she and Bernard experienced.

At least she had electricity, even if it was only a trickle that came in unpredictable spurts, lasting a few hours at most, if they were lucky. During those times, people worked hard to get done anything they could the old way, the easy way. Then, the electricity went out as abruptly as it came on, which to Nancy meant those who knew how to bring the power back online planned to keep it for themselves as long as they could.

A lot of their people enjoyed brewing a good cup of coffee when the power came on. God bless those special moments, too, because Nancy loved coffee, especially without all that grimy residue of grounds, thick as sludge at the bottom of the cup. Also, they could microwave food, making for much quicker meal preparation. Some women even took the time to bake as they had in the old days, but the items would go to waste if they didn't finish before the outage came. More important than any of this was the power tools were usable.

Their town resided along the Cuyahoga River, consisting only of a few dozen homes. Mere shacks compared to what many of them once lived in, the old-world homes seemed like mansions of the past, far too few of them still fully intact. The community worked to provide a haven and goods for the betterment of all its meager citizens. Bernard was a big part of that equation, and on a day when there was no power, his work would be slow going, thus harder than usual.

As he walked out the door, Nancy watched, noticing the way his eyes glanced up to the bright blue sky. She had forgotten, or tried to, all the things they endured. While those experiences served to bring them closer, they were awful memories to her. Even as the seeds of doubt were sown once more into her thoughts, her concern for the way Bernard stared in fascination at the cloudless heavens grew.

She saw the corners of his mouth turn up in a smile. Worse yet, she thought she heard him humming to himself as he walked down the road, perhaps oblivious to anything but an invisible voice in the sky. She looked at his fingers, seeing whether he was rubbing them together. He was, thankfully. This was a trick Marty taught them on the way to the battle at the hive. It meant Bernard was still there and not...something else.

On any other day Nancy may have gone to work herself. There was plenty of laundry and dishes to round up. It might upset the others if she didn't. But she detected something odd in the air today, a detail that held her back. Today, she needed to do something far more important than cleaning or cooking.

Nancy ran back into their shanty and tugged on her shoes. An act she now despised; she much preferred the feeling of the green grass between her toes. Simple things like that made her smile and think of better days.

She hurried out the door, following the path Bernard had taken, and scanned the horizon for signs of the large man. He far ahead of her, but she kept looking, being careful not let him see her. She didn't want him to know she was following him.

"G'day, Nancy." It was Martha Goodmore.

Nancy informed the woman to wait, holding up a single finger, but then ignored the woman and scurried along. Martha started to say something, but Nancy was too busy to worry about what anyone had to say right then. She supposed it was only a reminder of the daily chores she was now shirking. Nancy couldn't be bothered with such minute details at the moment.

After ten minutes, Nancy reached the end of their little town. That was where she expected to find Bernard, and as she made her way around the fence they had been building, she considered what he would say when he saw her. She didn't really care. She could always make up something and ran through excuses in her head, trying to think of a fitting one to use when Bill Cadry interrupted her.

"How goes it, Nancy?" She studied him for a second, unsure how she should answer. Her thoughts were elsewhere.

She nodded, and a funny scrunched up look appeared on his face. It was as if he hadn't been able to interpret her response. Nancy smiled, hoping to ease whatever doubt he had—a little sugar always made things better. *You can catch more flies with honey than vinegar,* her mother always told her.

"Haven't seen Bernie around today," Bill said. "Any idea where he might be? We kind of need him to help with this outer wall."

"He's not here?" Seeing how surprised Bill looked, Nancy decided it best to stick up for her man, just in case. "He has to be here somewhere. I followed him here."

Bill shook his head. A nervous laugh followed. "Maybe I just missed him. So, what brings you all the way out here?"

"Me? Just something I forgot to tell him. Something personal. Would you mind if I looked around for him?"

"Well, Nancy—"

She knew he was fishing for the *real* reason for her being here. He would know she wasn't where she belonged.

"It's important."

Bill went to ask but stopped himself. "Go ahead, Nan. Anyone bothers you, tell 'em I said it's okay."

Nancy rushed forward and gave Bill a little hug. "Thanks, Bill." He smiled and went back to work. The wall was starting to come around, but it was far from finished. She knew they would need it to keep out vagrants.

Nancy drifted along the outer edge of the men. Their hammers echoed down the river, as if the flow of the water was almost carrying those sounds away from their encampment. Saws gobbled up wood and men grunted, filling the morning air with the noise of hard work and body odor, the way God intended. But she didn't see Bernard anywhere.

She scanned the area outside of town and found a rocky embankment downstream. There, she glimpsed Bernard's head among the rocks. Taking large strides, she made it halfway to the rocks in seconds. After such a distance, her breathing quickened, even after Nancy slowed. As she neared him, she saw Bernard leaning against the rocks, staring up at the sky. Closer yet, she saw the way he had his legs pulled tight to his body, his arms hugging them close. He rocked back and forth in slow movements, always peering upward.

"Bernard?" He didn't answer. She came within twenty yards of him and called again. "Bernard?" When no response came, Nancy came within a few feet of him and tried again. "Bernard, honey?"

"Nancy?" He rubbed his fingers together frantically, working the invisible object he held there to the bone. Deep in thought, he appeared more troubled than ever. He looked back at her, tears streaming down his cheeks. Seeing this, Nancy felt like crying.

She dropped to her knees, taking his busy hands in her own to settle them. "What's wrong, Bernard?"

He looked up to the sky, then back to Nancy. His eyes trailed off to the sky once more. He stared for a long moment in complete silence. She waited, expecting the worst.

"They've come to take their children home."

Chapter 4

"No fair, Jakey."

A smile spread across Jake's face as he eyed his little brother, Marty. He loved the kid, but whenever they played this game, Jake wanted to win. After all, winning was everything.

"Is, too, Marty!" Jake extended his forefinger and thumb in the shape of an "L" and held it to his forehead. "Now stop being such a loser."

"Why do you always get to be the stronger country?"

There were so many ways to justify his actions. He could mention the simple fact that he was older. Or he could reference how much bigger he was than Marty. Those were the obvious reasons. But this was more than just childhood rivalry to Jake. A need swelled up inside of him, one that wanted fed. Marty could never understand. Jake needed to be superior to Marty, at least here, in this game. Marty excelled at everything else, both school and sports. Their parents even treated Marty better than Jake. That was why Jake needed this so bad, to have one thing over Marty. The fact it chapped Marty's ass whenever Jake won this game only made him want it more.

"Come *on*," Marty said.

Jake never budged. He would smack Marty upside the head, and then he would play-wrestle his brother into submission. Marty's little nation would always succumb to Jake's country. That was how Jake was back then, and even now part of Jake— that which identified as the Infinite—very much still wanted to come out on top. Remembering those days fondly, the Infinite tapped a finger on the side of the glass of water sitting in front of him. He had no need for the drink.

"Son, if I'm being honest—" Dave's abrupt words broke the Infinite out of a trance-like state filled with memories of his many wins. "I've never seen a man come down from the sky like that, the way you did back there."

"Why yes," the Infinite said. He let a thin smile curl upon his lips, having no intention of entertaining the man's annoying questioning. "I would imagine you haven't."

"He's Christ Almighty, Dave, come to take us home."

"Carol, please." Guilt appeared to overcome Dave, as he eyed up the Infinite nervously, perhaps thinking a bolt of lightning might strike him down. Even then, the threat of being smote wasn't enough to keep Dave from shooting his wife an uncomfortable scowl.

The Infinite could tell that the old man was swaying in his beliefs. They would both be followers.

"Listen," Dave said, "we have little, but if you are who we think you are, we'll help. For now, though, there are some clothes in back. Might run a little tight, but it's about all we got, and you should cover up some."

"Why, that will do fine, Dave." The Infinite smiled and stood.

Dave was staring at his neck. "Holy— I didn't notice before, son, but you got one bugger of a scar across your neck."

While Dave's wide eyes explored the scar, the Infinite did not try to hide it. However, he was growing tired of being looked at like this. It kind of angered him. If it didn't go against his plan, he would have done what he wanted to do and smote the man where he stood.

Dave hummed. "Looks like someone tried to take your head off."

Carol stood in a corner, still worshipping the Infinite. He liked the praise. It reminded him of his true place. The Infinite wanted her to pray to him. He needed it. It fed the anger in his heart. Once Marty was at his side, everything would be complete—and this other part of him finally satisfied. The human part. Together, his brother and he would rule the universe. Much praise to the Infinite.

The Infinite turned and went to the bedroom. When the doorknob turned, it instantly transported him back to Marty's old bedroom in his mind. He remembered peeking through that old keyhole, seeing Marty's face on the other side, how frightened he had looked. It brought a smile to the Infinite, a memory he savored still.

Then he remembered when Marty intruded on the Infinite's room. When his brother killed the first of the Infinite's many offspring. That was a bad memory, one that still stung him deeply, at the core of his very being. He would make many more children—already had, in fact.

Won't that surprise Marty.

The Infinite took in the old clothes lying across the bed. They were reminiscent of the clothes he once wore as a farmer. Back then, he tilled fields. Now, he was a reaper of men. Or, in a more familiar way, he was a fisher of men. He needed clothes before he could venture out, but these clothes wouldn't do. He wanted to make an impression on Bernard and his people.

He sat on the edge of the bed, considering that when he heard it for the first time. The network was so weak, the Infinite having to struggle to push thoughts or even read any of the others, just like it had been back on the ship. He couldn't focus on any one person—unable to locate them with any precision. Without doubt, some force had pulled him to this area. That much was undeniable. But he had to work hard to get even the slightest whisper out of his mind at the moment.

Then, drowning out a sea of a thousand voices, he heard a single whisper, and recognized the voice right away. The Infinite had been searching for the owner of this voice ever since the attack on the hive. His inability to uncover her had long troubled him. On the ship, that voice said only one thing, over and over, unceasingly. Now it said something different, albeit familiar.

"Marty," the voice said, again and again.

Chapter 5

At first, Nancy was unsure of what she *thought* she saw. Having shirked their daily work, she was quite happy having Bernard asleep in bed for some much-needed rest. While he slept, she sat out front on an old aluminum-folding chair, observing the stars. It was one of the few things she still enjoyed about the evening sky. Interrupting the relaxing moment, she saw something move from the corner of her eye. Unable to discern what it was, she peered down the dirt road.

Her eyes discovered Tia May. Tia sat in front of her shanty much like Nancy, unmoving and maybe even asleep. Then Nancy saw it again, what looked like a person. Not just any person, though. This person was wearing very little or not a stitch of clothing at all.

Nancy's thoughts ran wild. After Bernard's scare earlier today, panic took hold. Might this be the alien race returning to take Bernard away from her again? She had needed to work hard to forget about the aliens, but now it was more difficult than ever to let go of such a thought.

With sudden resolve, she rose to her feet, ready to take on the world. She would defend her man; would confront a whole horde of aliens before she let them take him away. They wouldn't succeed, not now, never again.

Staring down the dirt road, she searched for unusual movement. There was nothing but a light breeze, making her feel natural for the first time since the bad days. She heard nothing but Tia's light snoring and saw only the stars twinkling in the night sky.

Nancy laughed, shrugging off her paranoia. Why would they come back? They had what they came for. There was no reason for them to return. Her nervous laugh consumed her, making her feel as though she was lying to herself. She tried to ignore the notion, thinking it might be better to get to bed now before she ruminated on this any further.

Turning to the door, she huffed out loud, reiterating her frustration of the unknown, and went to grab the knob. Before her hand reached it, a woman ran in front of her, causing Nancy's heart to twist inside of her chest like a dishtowel being wrung. The woman, with dark strands of tangled hair dangling in front of her wild eyes, grabbed Nancy's shoulders and shook. Nancy didn't stir from her daze, and the woman shook her again.

"Is he here?" the woman said.

Nancy didn't answer, too stunned by the sudden appearance of the woman standing in front of her, trying to figure out what she needed to do to protect Bernard.

"Nancy, is he here?"

"Who are you?" Nancy's voice wavered, struggling to get the words out. "You can't have Bernard!"

"What? Did he come for Marty?"

"How do you know who Marty is?" Nancy examined the gaunt woman, noticing how her skin clung tight to her body, revealing every rib, every bone. This was a woman who hadn't eaten well in a long time. She looked anorexic, starved. Worse yet, the woman seemed crazy, disturbed, out of her mind.

"Is he here?" The woman licked her lips, appearing anxious over Nancy's inability to answer. The woman shook her again, trying to force out an answer.

"Who? Bernard?"

"No, Nancy."

The woman shook her again, forcing Nancy to look into her eyes. Nancy saw something familiar in those dark pools, something she would never forget. Those were eyes she once hated.

"Sandy?" Nancy's heart plummeted at the realization of who this woman was. She took a step back, felt her blood boiling inside as she thought about what the woman once did to hurt the man she loved. After all this time, it was still so difficult not to see the gun in her hands, and Bernard lying there dying. But she also remembered this woman had helped them.

"Shush!" Sandy looked around as if struck by paranoia herself. "Is he here?"

"Who, Sandy?" Nancy stepped forward, removing her sweater. She swung it around Sandy, hoping it might calm her down some. It didn't seem to help.

"Jake?" Sandy said. "Has Jake been here yet?"

Nancy stared at the crusty lips of a woman. Sandy had just spoken the words she most feared. So, Marty's brother was coming, just as Bernard had predicted. Nancy froze, a cold shudder tingling throughout her body, and though Sandy kept speaking, she found herself unable to hear the words.

Chapter 6

Ike gave Becca a look, hoping she would take the hint and join Bento outside. He didn't trust any dog around his crops. Never mind the fact the dog might eat something, but Ike also had a knack for discovering piles of poo by stepping right in them. And Ike didn't want landmines to end up all over his property because, with his luck, he would step in every single last one before they dried up.

She didn't leave, though, and the conversation made him uncomfortable right from the start. There were things from his past he didn't want to discuss in front of Becca. Now he would have no choice. Hadn't she seen enough to know what those things might be? She had lived through as much of this as Ike had. Realizing this, he turned back to Marty.

Marty looked thinner. He still had that muscular build from his days of being a full-time farmer, but he looked leaner. His hair was longer, too, hanging down to his shoulders. The gray locks curled at the ends, framing his peppered beard. His steely eyes also appeared different, more focused perhaps. It was almost as if Marty had shaved a few hard years off and somehow ended up being younger.

Ike watched as Marty removed something from his back—a sheathed sword. Marty took the time to unstrap a holster, freeing the gun at his hip. Obviously, there was more that had changed about Marty than Ike realized upon first glance. "So, what? You some sort a fucking ninja cowboy now or what?"

Marty grinned and sat at the table, upright and proper. His eyes trained on Ike, searching his feelings. Then Marty's lips parted, and he let out a hearty laugh. "Hardly."

Thankfully, it seemed this was the same old Marty Ike remembered.

"Then why you carrying that damn over-sized butcher's knife around? And a pistola to boot?"

Becca placed a steamy cup of coffee in front of Marty. She leaned over and gave him a small kiss on the cheek. Ike could hear her whisper how good it was to see him again. Yes, it was good to see his friend after all this time.

"Never can be too sure nowadays." Marty's eyes rolled suggestively up toward the sky. Ike understood the sentiment well. Unfortunately, they hadn't killed them all. Following their adventure, Bernard shared the fact that he believed Marty's brother hadn't been a casualty of their battle. So it made sense that Marty would want to be ready in case he got another opportunity to kill his brother. Ike supposed the dog was only an added extra measure of protection.

An uncomfortable silence grew between them, as he feared the direction the conversation would take, one of desperation. Ike didn't want any part of a discussion like that. He had a woman now and this alone, if nothing else, would keep him out of any business regarding those alien fuckos. Ike's brief stint as a hero was over the moment their battle ended. Knowing this about himself, he wanted to sway the conversation to something more to his liking.

"I sure wish I would've paid more attention to your damn farming lessons, Marty."

Marty didn't respond. His eyes gleamed, making Ike feel anxious.

A bead of sweat rolled down Ike's forehead. He tried again.

"How's Sheila doing, Old Boy?" Ike leaned forward, took his own cup of coffee in hand. "She all right, buddy?"

A light howl came from outside the door. Marty ignored it, his focus trained on Ike. Keeping his silence, Marty took a sip of the coffee and then nodded to Becca, indicating it was a good cup. He turned back to Ike, still wearing that grin. The smile on Ike's face subsided.

"I left her alone at the farm," Marty finally said. He paused, took another meager sip. "I had to. She's changed these last couple days, if you know what I mean."

"No, what do you mean?" Becca's eyebrows rose from both surprise and curiosity. "Different?"

Now Ike wished more than ever she had taken his cue to leave the two of them alone. The tension mounted fast. Although Ike very much liked Marty, this conversation was over long before it really got going. There were better things to talk about, and Ike couldn't help Marty. Not anymore. He wouldn't help him. There was too much at stake.

Marty looked at Becca, then back to Ike. "She's been wandering off a lot as of late. She stares up at the stars and doesn't say much about it, but I know why. What do you think, Ike?"

Those words stung Ike. "Ah hell, Marty. Why are you getting your panties in a bunch over this shit?"

Ike stood and walked over to Becca. He maneuvered his body in a way to usher Becca toward the other room. She didn't take to his suggestion, sidestepping him, and taking a place beside Ike.

"Oh, what the hell?" Ike flung his hands up. "Maybe she just likes the goddamn stars, Marty." But even Ike had heard the hitch in his voice. He didn't really believe what he had suggested at all.

Ike tracked Becca's movement at his side.

Marty set his coffee down and pushed his chair back. When he did, Ike glimpsed a ponytail.

Christ, Marty's gone all hippie on me.

Isn't that some shit, right there?

Marty stood and approached Ike and Becca. Things got crowded fast, and Ike felt overcome by an urge to retreat outside, into the open air. Such a confined space could be strangling.

"You know the truth." Marty placed a hand on Ike's shoulder, his touch almost electric. Hell yeah, Ike knew the truth, but he had too much to lose now. Before, it had only been his sorry ass he needed to worry about. That had been little to risk. Now he had Becca. But how could he relay this to Marty without sounding like a pansy ass? He couldn't.

Ike moved to the other side of the room, edging around Marty, leaving his old friend standing beside the woman he loved. He walked over to the sword and examined it. Some Asian writing ran the length of the scabbard. A red ribbon wound around it several times, ending in an unfamiliar knot. "I can't—"

"Before you say anything more, Ike, remember what we are up against. This affects all of us. Not just me. They want us all."

"I know." Ike wasn't sure this was the entire truth, though. "It's—"

"What is it, Ike?" Becca asked.

Marty eyed up Becca, seeming to understand Ike's conflict instantly. A caring smile spreading across Marty's face.

Becca looked to Marty for the answer Ike wasn't able to provide. Ike tossed the words around in his head, trying to figure out a proper explanation, but hadn't landed on anything good. Marty saved him the trouble.

"He's afraid of losing you, my dear."

Becca's face flushed. It was true. Sure, they never had an official marriage, but their union was no different for Ike.

Ike extended his hand to her. "You're the only thing I've ever cared about in my sorry ass life."

Marty shifted, allowing the space needed for Becca to make her way to Ike. She moved slow and graceful, took his hand in hers, pulling the rigid man into her arms. Letting go like this, Ike didn't feel so tough anymore. She placed her hands on his cheeks and pulled his head to her shoulder.

Marty stepped forward and put his hand on Ike's back.

Ike turned his head to glance at him from Becca's shoulder, tears stinging his eyes. He hated that he was fucking crying.

"It's okay, Ike," Marty said. "I get it. I understand everything. Believe me."

Ike believed him. He knew what Marty had endured.

Becca pulled Ike in closer, nesting her mouth to his ear. Her whispers were warm and tickled, her breath sweet. "I love you, but your friend needs you right now."

He had to help. Knew he would even. For now, though, he didn't want to leave the comfort of this house. The safety of Becca's embrace. It had been so...*good*. He owed Marty for helping him find this life. And here was Becca urging him on.

"Ah, fuck!" Ike wiped the single tear from his eye. He tried to play if off by acting all tough. "If I'm going to help you, I'd better have a gun, too. And not one of those wussy type pistols you been carrying around like a sissy."

Marty grinned. "I'd expect no less."

"I need a big gun. And no damn ninja sword for me, either. I'm no freaking ninja."

"I know, Ike."

Becca smiled at Ike. He realized then this was the right decision. She would be here waiting for him when he got back. And he *would* come back. It would be best if she stayed as far away from this shit as she could, too. But Ike worried how far this new issue might reach.

"Let's rest for the night." Marty took a seat again and sipped, enjoying the coffee. "Tomorrow we head for Bernard."

"Ah, crap." An uncomfortable smile found Ike's face. "We're bringing the frigging human transistor radio with us?"

Chapter 7

To Nancy, Sandy seemed like she was on the verge of insanity. Sandy kept fidgeting, looking as though she had lost some control over her fingers, as if she were on some high dose of medication. Every so often, one of Sandy's hands would just flail outward, as if the nerves had gotten so bunched up the hand no choice but to release that energy. Each time this happened, Sandy would study Nancy, as if expecting a reaction, her facial expressions giving away just how aware she was of the issues she was experiencing and how they must look. Both Bernard and Nancy said nothing, though, focusing on Sandy's story more than the physical hitches.

Sandy rucked one hand under the other, perhaps trying to steady herself some. "It was the most alone I've ever felt."

"Where did you go, Sandy?" Bernard said.

She regarded him, and for a moment, Nancy believed there was some secret understanding between the two. Why wouldn't there be? Obviously, Bernard remained tethered to the alien network. Wouldn't Sandy be, too? And judging by what Sandy described of her time on that ship, she had developed the ability to put herself into the very stream Bernard found himself unable to break free from. Nancy knew that with Jake's return, Sandy could answer all Bernard's questions without using her vocal cords. Thankfully, Sandy didn't leave Nancy out of the loop.

"Who knows how far we traveled?" Sandy huffed. "A lot can happen in that span of time."

Up to this point of the story, Sandy had been living on the

alien ship for most of the year as a stowaway. They had discovered her only once and upon her capture, they had capsulized her in one of the hive's coffin-like cells just like Bernard had been back when they battled the aliens the first time. But it hadn't affected Sandy in the same way as Bernard, as they connected her to the alien network back during her time stationed in the underground military facility.

"What did you eat?" Nancy asked.

Sandy regarded Nancy with a sullen face. She didn't look like she wanted to answer. Why would she want to avoid that question? Sandy's hands clasped together, released, then the fingers interlocked once again. A clear look of disgust struck her gaunt face.

"You don't really want to know if I'm being honest." Sandy stared at the ground. Her malnourished cheeks flushed. "Most of it wasn't of this Earth."

Nancy thought she saw Sandy gag a little. She considered what lengths Sandy would go through to fulfill her mission. This was the woman's burden, her curse. She would never give up, no matter what she had to do. What she had to *eat*. Nancy instantly conjured up images of some gross things. The idea a woman like Sandy could get in the mindset to eat something worse than those aberrations sickened her. That said, the part of her that remembered what Sandy once did to her Bernard, reveled in those thoughts. Even if that made her feel a little guilty.

"So, you felt it, too?" Bernard asked.

Nancy didn't want to ask. She had her own feelings on the matter after seeing what Bernard had done, heard the things he said. She wanted no part of this. Though it would be Bernard who determined where they went from here, being the one most affected by all of this.

"No," Sandy said.

Bernard wore an expression of surprise. "You couldn't feel it?"

"No," she said, reiterating the fact. "Things worked a little different on the ship. The network isn't the same. It's more like a fishbowl within the bigger scope of things. And within that environment was a single brooding voice."

"What about their planet?" Nancy asked.

"They don't have one. Not anymore. They don't even need one. Their ship runs off the energy the hives produce, and the ship itself is large enough to house an entire civilization and more. Until recently, they were a dying race. Marty's brother changed everything."

Sandy reached for the bowl in front of her with both hands shaking. She ignored the spoon and raised the entire bowl of soup to her dried lips. As she slurped, the spoon handle worked its way along the edge of the bowl until it struck her right nostril. Sandy didn't appear to notice, too caught up in the taste of real food.

Bernard looked as though he wanted to say something. Nancy watched his eyes twitch, perhaps rethinking his words. An expression of clarity spread across his face, as though he had gained all the information he wanted. Had they been communicating subconsciously after all? Nancy wondered how much of the conversation she missed.

"Let me get you something else, Sandy." Nancy got up, the frustration of being left out of this conversation overwhelming her. As she walked to the cupboard, she glanced back. They were definitely talking in their special way. It was unnerving.

Nancy reached into one cabinet and pulled out some crackers. They were rather old and a little stale, but it was food. She dipped a cup in the large pot, getting Sandy a fresh glass of water.

"And what of Marty's brother?" Nancy said over her shoulder.

Sandy looked at her as if she had gone backwards in the conversation. Then, as if the woman hadn't realized what they had been doing, Sandy appeared embarrassed. This confirmed Nancy's suspicions.

"I'm so sorry, Nancy. I haven't used my real voice in quite some time. It's—"

"Don't worry, dear." Somehow, Nancy found an appreciation for the young woman, almost a motherly instinct. Having no children of her own, Nancy liked that association more than she could express in words.

Sandy face lost some color. "Jake is much more powerful than ever."

"Powerful?" A revolting taste spread in Nancy's mouth.

"Yes, he can do things. Special things. And above all else, I think seeing him this time will be very hard on Marty." She looked at both of them, swallowed a cracker whole, and took a large drink of water. With her mouth full of food, she continued. "We *have* to help Marty."

Chapter 8

Sheila sat on the roof of a car, snuggled deep into the old fluffy chair they had placed there long ago. The car no longer worked and with this bit of extra height, Marty and she had a great view of the sunset. This simple place meant more to her than anything because of the time they had shared.

She didn't like Marty being off on his own or even leaving the farm. Though she understood he had his reasons, there were some daily chores she couldn't handle on her own. It was more about his timing. She didn't know where he went, but she had a good idea why. He had been planning for so long, but he hadn't followed through with his scheme. He likely did not know she had discerned any part of his complex strategy.

But he would have noticed the look in her face. He might have glimpsed that a few days back, when the time grew near. Marty would have known something needed done, and he would have been proactive about it. Would have made sure he had his ducks in a row long before any of this started.

Her auburn hair fluttered into her face. She ignored the way it tickled her nose. Little things like this gave her such pleasure now.

Once the network became audible to her again, she believed Marty had confirmed what he long suspected about Sheila in that moment; that she remained tied to that network somehow. They never talked about what happened much. They didn't have to. She understood Marty's feelings on the matter because of the way Marty he watched over her. And he had been there to catch her glaring up at the stars the other night.

Marty had secrets, too, though. Not traits of his personality, like one might expect. They had found plenty of time to share those details with one another. Those were the good days. Now that he had left, the bad days would soon come.

Where did Marty go? To see Bernard? She didn't think he would bother with Bernard, who could connect to the network as well. He might want to talk to Nancy perhaps, but she thought it more likely he went to see Ike. If so, would Ike even try to him help? She doubted this, too. Ike always had been a selfish man. Whatever Marty saw in the man, she did not.

Maybe Marty was strong enough to defeat the aliens on his own. He had somewhat mastered the art of sword fighting, having studied under some random wanderer he had met in town. When Marty wasn't working on the farm, he was training. He had put on muscle, too, looking so much stronger than he had back when they first met. So maybe he went on alone.

Sheila wished he had left Bento. Their well-disciplined dog, a lab, listened to Marty's every command. Though the dog took up more of Marty's time than she cared for, she would feel safer with Bento around. Any animosity she felt toward the dog wasn't jealousy at all, so much as it was that she didn't want to have to compete for Marty's time. But it was also more than that, too. Bento could see inside her. The dog had sensed the network upon its return, the dog's ears had twitched every time she got close. It was almost like one of those whistles only a dog could hear. And as the signal strengthened, Bento's reactions changed, occasionally growling and sometimes even barking at her.

Without doubt, Bento had her number. Sheila suspected this was the very reason Marty searched for a dog to begin with. Most of the domestic animals ran free and unseen nowadays, but Marty had spent looking for what he referred to as "the right one." Once he found Bento, he worked for hours on end to train the dog. Bento picked up things fast, too, more so than an average dog.

She sometimes wondered how Marty found any the time for her at all. Yet, night after night, he always did. Never forced, either. Every minute he spent with her was more valuable than any possession. He loved her. She knew it in her heart. Love for him filled her heart. She loved how devoted he was, how disciplined he had become. He was a leader at the worst of times. She even loved this newest transformation of Marty, the over thinker. He had planned for this second coming, and, upon its arrival, he hadn't even hesitated.

Or did he?

On the horizon, a flicker of lightning heated the sky. A small, dark cloud dirtied the orange-hued sunset. She tried not to focus on the storm, although she worried it might spoil the moment. Then, as if someone were answering her prayers, the clouds dispersed.

Sheila grinned and folded her hands over her stomach. She hugged herself. Life could be so beautiful. She observed the sunset without a care in the world. For now, the network was quiet, and that was a good thing. She hoped Marty was safe and prayed to see him soon. With this last thought, Sheila drifted into a slumber.

Chapter 9

Marty woke early, long before anyone else. He strapped his sword to his back—the one he would use to kill his brother, should the opportunity arise again—and being careful not to wake anyone, hurried to the front door. He suspected the conflict with his brother would come sooner, given Sheila's recent behavior. This time alone was more necessary than ever so he could meditate and realign his focus.

Walking along the edge of the fields, Marty admired Ike's handiwork. His gardens weren't pretty, but they were good enough to put food on the table. Given enough time, Ike would likely hone his skills. Ike was a capable man, fully able to discover things on his own. Maybe one day he would learn to see the amateur mistakes, like those that led to pint-sized corn. Marty observed the rows, how close together they were, and laughed. Ike would figure it all out.

Manhood was something a man learned through teaching. Yes, having a good role model never hurt, but Marty believed it was more something one stumbled upon as they neared manhood. And a young man learned to define those traits over time, growing and evolving into it. Ike may have had a late start, but it would come to him. Marty had faith in that.

Plenty of men had fumbled for a firm grasp of the ability once they found it. One could spend hours nurturing that knowledge, trying to cultivate it at will. For some, it took longer than it did others. For Ike, it had taken half a lifetime, but hone this skill he would. Someday he would master these fields, too. In his own time.

Marty didn't want to cheat Ike the experience, but he would lend a hand. He waded into the fields, his fingers dangling through what foliage they could reach. He found a small patch of seedlings and weeded out several of the plants with haste, allowing for the proper space between the plants so they had room to grow. All life ever needed was room to grow. Ike would see this soon enough.

He stood, eyeing his dirty work. It wouldn't do.

Marty picked up the plucked plants and carried them far down the hillside. There, he hid them under some loose brush. Ike would never appreciate the knowledge if he thought Marty led him right to it. Marty didn't want to interfere with Ike's personal growth. He only wanted to guide him to the correct path.

Traveling back up the hillside, he stopped near the top. The ground wasn't level so that made it difficult to stand, but it would serve his purposes well. The entire world felt askew as of late.

His eyes searched for Bento. He spotted the dog lying on his back, his naughty bits hanging free. Marty had become attached to the dog. Joy overwhelmed him to think he had stumbled upon the very dog he had been searching for. It had been a pleasant surprise, all things considered.

Staring off at the sunrise, Marty focused his thoughts. He squinted, as if trying to burn a hole right through the sun's fiery core. When his heart slowed to the right pace, Marty drew his sword from its scabbard. When the tip found the end of its sheath, he flicked the sword forward, and the blade rang to attention.

Chapter 10

What Ike saw Marty doing was some real fucking Kung Fu shit. As the thought occurred to Ike, he reflected on years of watching Kung Fu Theater every Sunday afternoon as a child. He could have watched those cheesy movies all day long. Now was no different.

He remembered one movie where a guy thrust his hand right through some bozo's skull. The camera had panned out to show the man's fingers wiggling through to the other side, an uncomplicated scheme to make the scene appear authentic. It hadn't worked, and all those splendid movies were all gone now. This, however, was the real deal.

I wonder if Marty could put his hand through Jake's skull.

Probably not.

Bento yawned, gawking at Ike. He returned the gesture, noticing how Bento positioned himself, letting his junk hang out in the open. Ike envied the damn creature. What he wouldn't give to lie around sunning his scrotum all day. He had work to tend to, and he didn't want Becca doing his chores for him. She would, too, if he let her.

He looked back at Marty. Marty's hand twisted the blade forward and a light ring of steel struck the sky. The noise surprised Ike. He hadn't thought such a thing possible, except in the movies. Marty's arms moved like a dancer. His knees bent, and Ike expected his old friend might break into an Irish jig. Rising to his tippy-toes with true ballet form, Marty froze.

The urge to laugh overwhelmed Ike. But he went on with his day, ignoring the pose.

After a few minutes, it amazed Ike to see Marty was still in the same pose. Then, as if sensing Ike's gaze, Marty thrust his sword out, cutting through nothingness. The noise the sword made caused Ike to wonder whether Marty had somehow split the air molecules.

Marty struck another pose, looking somewhat like a flamingo caught in prayer. One leg folded up, his foot sideways against his other knee, it made Ike cringe in discomfort. Thankfully, the urge to go to the bathroom took priority over Marty's Kung Fu show. On his way to the can, Ike monitored what Marty was doing, though.

Again, holding the pose, Marty shot the sword out. It cut through the sky, the sound of it so much louder than Ike expected. This time, when the sword reached its ending place, it wavered in the morning sky. A glimmering beauty. But so was a good bowel movement.

Ike grabbed a random newspaper from his personal stash. He had discovered them among the remains of someone's garage. This edition was from three years ago. He folded it behind him and stuck it in the back of his jeans as he headed to the outhouse.

This had been one of the few pleasantries of this new life Ike didn't enjoy. Having to empty the shitter now and then made for the most dreadful work, even if most of the waste was your own. He enjoyed the seat he kept fastened to the hole, though, one of the nicer ones. Despite feeling a little guilty about just taking it from a local hardware store, he doubted anyone would mind.

As his cheeks found the soft stuffed plastic seat, a light burst of air escaped the cushion. Then a bigger, more invasive air escaped Ike.

Ike unfolded the paper, but only got through first line before an interruption halted everything. The dog barked, repeatedly. The urge to yell at the dog to stop overcame him, but he held his tongue. But he couldn't read a word with all that racket.

Then, despite all the noise, Ike heard a familiar voice, and felt a sudden urgency. Whatever made the dog bark like that couldn't be good. He needed to find out why anyone would come all the way out here. Were they here for Ike or for Marty? Once again, Ike found himself involved in all the wrong ways, at the wrong dang time.

Chapter 11

The trip had not been easy for the Infinite, in large because of Dave's incessant doubting and questions. As they approached the outskirts of Bernard's town, the Infinite was sure it wouldn't be long before they drew the attention of its residents. That was, if Dave didn't alert them first with all his babbling.

"Son, you could have picked out more than my wife's tablecloth to wear, you know?"

Yes, the Infinite knew this. But dressing in regular clothes would negate his plan. He had reasons for wearing this garb. A purpose beyond even what his alien cohorts knew about. Only his plan mattered. Fuck free will. The Infinite's will be done.

Within him, something grumbled against this blasphemous thought. Some old part of him didn't like the sound of it so much; Jake, of course. The Infinite would silence that half once Marty stood at his side. Then all would be appeased, and it would be hail the Infinite and his wisdom.

For the moment, he listened to his thoughts, expecting to hear Jake's complaints again. A calming sensation fell over him knowing his brother was nearby. The fact he needed his brother had been something he had long denied back when he was just Jake. Now, he—no, they—must have Marty by their side.

"Dave, you're gonna to get the wrath of God if you keep talking like that." Carol bowed to the Infinite.

That was true regardless of whether or not the man shut his mouth. The Infinite fully planned to rid himself of the man first chance he got. But there was something refreshing about her submissive tone. It had been quite some time since he felt so powerful. But there was no time for that now. After this was over and he was back on the ship—his ship—he could enjoy the satisfaction then.

"Sorry," Dave said.

An apology meant little to the Infinite at this point. Dave could say anything he wanted at this point. This would end the same way no matter what anyone said. There would be no free will. No thinking for one's self. The Infinite would do it all for Dave and everyone else.

This made the Infinite smile, but he said nothing.

"It's just that I don't understand why a boy would want to be all naked is all," Dave said, "choosing what you did when there were plenty of good clothes to choose from."

"Dave, hush now." Carol shot him a look as if he were the antichrist himself. He wasn't. The Infinite had that covered.

"What're we doing in this town, anyway?" Yet another question from Dave.

This one annoyed the Infinite more than the others. It made him wish he could invoke his will right now. But he had to wait. If he didn't, his plan wouldn't be as effective. Then, as suddenly as the thought came to him, the townspeople came into view, and the Infinite prepared to unleash his fury upon Dave.

A short man called out in their direction. "I'm Bill Cadry. Can we help you folks?"

The Infinite didn't answer. Neither did Carol. The people of this small town drew closer, and the Infinite turned his attention to Dave.

"We could use some food if you don't mind," Dave said.

The Infinite saw visions of his brother and him playing as children. Memories like this bothered him, as they stole time from him, made him remember things he didn't want to, brought up weird feelings.

That's just Jake thinking.

The part of himself wanted to stop the Infinite from the inside, but Jake wouldn't be successful. The Infinite lifted a hand, palm exposed to Dave.

Dave stopped. "What? We don't want food?"

An orange glow emitted from the Infinite's hand as he thrust it at Dave. A beam of orange energy shot through Dave's stomach, tearing a large hole in his belly. Dave was in too much shock to react, the pain clear in his expression.

Carol fell to the ground sobbing. The townspeople lifted their guns preparing to battle. All of it pleased the Infinite.

"What are you doing?" one woman asked.

"Quiet, Tia!" Bill lifted his gun.

"Do not be afraid." The Infinite moved toward Dave with grace, a gentle nature to his step. Dave remained afoot, still in shock, looking as though struck by lightning. A row of guns found the Infinite, tracking his every movement, ready to drop him. Dave was dying, but a human death was such a trivial matter. The Infinite had learned much of himself since Marty tried to kill him, and one little trick would convince these sheep of everything he needed them to believe.

"Now, you hold it right there, Mister," Bill said. "I don't know what you are or what you want, but we don't want your kind in our town. Now, get!"

The Infinite placed his hands over the huge opening in Dave's stomach. He whispered soft prayers from a book he once read in another life, loud enough for all to hear. Speaking quietly was unnecessary, but it brought a certain realness to this work. The Infinite's hands glowed bright orange, pulsing on Dave's belly. His hands flickered, then a bright flash sent Dave's arms and legs outward just like Jake had once experienced before he became the Infinite.

When the Infinite removed his hands, those closest townsfolk gasped in disbelief. Tears of joy replaced the sadness imprinted on Carol's cheeks. She stared at Dave with surprise. Dave didn't appear to notice the miraculous healing, mostly because the Infinite had tied Dave into the network. Now the Infinite could express his will *through* Dave.

"It's a miracle!" Dave spun, making sure even those in the back could hear his joyous shouts. "A miracle, I tell you."

Carol echoed his sentiment agreeing. "Our Lord, the blessed Jesus, came back to save us."

A few had already fallen into this web, lowering their guns.

Others remained skeptical. In time, the Infinite would pull them all in, everyone he could find. They would be his people, believing what he willed. And when the time was right, they would all join the network.

The Infinite's will be done, indeed.

Chapter 12

"Bernard, honey, what is it?" Nancy asked.

Bernard stared off toward town, listening, but he couldn't discern what was making the sound. What he did know though, whatever had made that sound wasn't good. If he were in his right mind, they would hightail it out of there, but he was having trouble doing much of anything on his own these days. The network was getting stronger.

He had been correct when he told his friends he was a divided man. Part of him, the stronger of the two halves for now, wanted to make sure Nancy got out of there safe. But that other part of him was like a seed planted in early spring, growing faster than he preferred. That part of him wanted him to go back to town as soon as possible.

The network was different this time. Before, it had been a strong surge of energy, pulsing through him like the waves of wake a boat makes upon a lake. This time, the network was much weaker, as if the waves had long crashed against one another and started to settle. The signal seemed to diminish in strength.

Only, it never really did fade. The network didn't tail off or suddenly drop off altogether. It was always there, only suppressed. It was like attempting to tune in a distant radio station, a faint signal with a constant static that hindered his ability to do so. It was difficult to hear, and other times, he couldn't make out anything at all.

That was when Bernard realized he was fully trying to listen. That other part of him wanted to hear what was being said, to identify the source of the network. No, not just that other half. He also wanted to hear it, perhaps only to confirm it was happening and not just some memory his mind had conjured up.

In the network, he heard the echo of a single word. A word familiar to him, though he struggled to place where he had heard it before. Perhaps it was some residual memory, left behind from Jake's intrusion. He worried what that might mean. Was he crazy? Even more unusual was the fact this voice sounded a lot like Sandy. Over and over, in an endless loop, he heard her say the word "now."

Bernard searched for Sandy in the network, as it was much easier to hear her thoughts now that she was within proximity. But even Sandy was out of tune right now. Could she hear what he did? Her expression gave away nothing, and he couldn't help but notice how she studied him. Was she searching his thoughts and emotions as much as he was her?

What has she discovered?

Sandy was different. Somehow, she had mastered the ability to control the network. Perhaps she was one of them. Maybe she wasn't. Bernard couldn't tell, as he couldn't see anything she didn't want him to see. He was, however, certain that she had full privileges within his mental library.

She's too good at this game.

"What do you think, Bernard?" Nancy asked. "Okay to go on?"

He looked over at Sandy who sat on her horse. She didn't look like she was in a hurry.

Does she hear it, too? Maybe she longs to go to it.

"No?" Nancy asked.

He shook his head. "Huh?" Nancy came into focus through his daydreaming vision.

"You were shaking your head," Nancy said.

He thought for a moment, vaguely remembering the act. "I was just clearing my head."

"On, then," Sandy said. "Let's move."

Bernard looked at her with a dull expression. Her color had come back. She was healing faster than he'd expected she would. Soon, she would be strong enough to stop him, if he went against her. She would stand in his way if he went back. Unless, of course, she wanted to go with him.

Chapter 13

"Sheila, dear, wake up," a man's voice said.

She stirred, trying to ignore him.

"Wake up, honey."

"Not now, Marty."

She snuggled deeper into the comfort of the chair. A chill fell over her, so she pulled the cover up to her nose, trying to keep warm. The sensation spread to her legs, but she dared not let her stomach or chest become exposed, so she shrank into a ball, trying to cover her entire body with the cover.

"It's time, my dear."

"No, Marty. Please let me sleep."

The blanket was *so* soft, warmth seeming to radiate from it. She could feel the sun beginning to heat the world. Soon she wouldn't need the blanket.

"Wake up." The voice had a more demanding tone this time, and that was when Sheila became aware it hadn't been Marty.

She sat up and looked around. Her eyes struggled against the morning sun as it crested above the hillside, but she saw no one.

I wish Marty was here.

She felt no more chill but kept the blanket covering her.

Looking out over the fields, she considered it had been a nightmare. Perhaps, she was dreaming about Marty and the fact she missed him had caused—

Or had it been Jake she was dreaming about?

No, it was Marty.

Her fuzzy thinking was from more than just being tired. The

network kept ringing in her thoughts, and it seemed so much closer to her now. She could hear hints of the past, like little echoes. And she detected a presence in the network, coming from Jake, she believed. It was like a magnetic pull, but it was nothing like the previous time.

"Now," a voice said.

Sheila stood up and let the blanket fall to the roof of the car. The chair scraped the metal as it slid back a few inches in her haste.

"Who's there? Who is it?"

"It's time, Sheila." The voice was insistent, clarifying that none of this had been a dream.

"Time for what?"

"Wake up."

A new sensation surged through Sheila, a pulse of energy absorbed by her body. Her limbs shot out as she struggled to maintain it, unable to do anything but let it happen. She shook on top of the car as if struck by lightning. Something was searching her, scanning her thoughts for needed information. When it found what it wanted, it was as if all that energy was being sucked back into her body. Her arms dropped to her sides. She felt woozy and exhaled deeply. Her heart raced, forcing her to steady her breathing.

"Who is that?"

When she found out, she screamed inside her thoughts, not wanting it to be him, but the truth was far too obvious to ignore. Jake had returned, and he had found a way into her mind. She could sense him probing there, having flicked some mental switch within Sheila that put him in command of her body. Once thrown, something changed deep inside of her. A numbing sensation spread down her body, all the way to her toes. It felt like dozens of spiders, paralyzing her from the waist down.

Her heart beat like a wild drum in her chest as she struggled to remain calm. But try as she might, she could not keep this down. Yet all her thoughts and emotions remained, even as the numbing worked its way into her chest. Then her heart was all she felt, a distant rapping sound that was barely audible.

I'm changing.

Into what, she couldn't be sure. Whatever it was, it would be horrible. She remembered the horrid creatures they once fought and prayed she wouldn't become one of them. Her vision faded, and she found herself trapped within her own thoughts, being held captive in a whole other reality. She was being squashed out of existence with no idea how much of her true self would remain, if any at all.

Chapter 14

Marty glanced back over his shoulder in time to see Ike exit the outhouse. He hurried his way—fear stricken across his face, his pants clenched in a fist at his waist as Ike fumbled with the buttons. Marty couldn't help but laugh.

Ike was right, though. This was something concerning.

"So, you were saying?" Marty tugged at the scruff of his goatee with his thumb and forefinger.

"Your brother asked me to come find you. He requests you join him."

"What the fuck did you just say, numbnuts?" Ike stumbled over to where they were talking. He still hadn't gotten his jeans buttoned. "Who the fuck are you?"

"My name is Ron."

"Ron? Well whoop-te-friggin-doo! Yeah, I remember you, dickhead. What the fuck do you want, *Ron*?" The scowl on Ike's face said everything Ike felt about this surprise visit. "I think you better leave, if you know what's friggin' good for ya." Ike bent over, picked up a pitchfork, and thrust it out in a menacing way.

Marty knew Ike was only protecting Becca, but he was also being protective of Marty to a degree. A sense of brotherhood had grown between the two of them. He placed a hand on Ike's pitchfork and urged him to lower it with a gentle push.

Ike stared at him with disbelief but did as instructed.

"How did you even find us?" Ike asked. "Who told you where the hell I live? Have you got some sort of fucking bug planted around here somewhere?"

Ron looked past Marty at the dog. Ike did, too, but he doubted

Ike would figure out why anyone would be so interested in a dog. No one had bugged the dog. Besides, Marty knew as much as Ike did that other people in their lives knew where he lived. If Jake controlled those people, then he would know.

Marty returned his eyes to their visitor. "I'm sorry, Ron, but we have things to do. So, if you wouldn't mind telling my brother, we shan't be attending."

Ron only stared at Marty. If he made one wrong move, Marty would take his head. He had already prepared for that.

"He thought you'd say as much." Ron brushed his clothes, perhaps a nervous habit. "He said to tell you he has Sheila."

Of course, he does.

Marty had considered that possibility for a long time now. He had tossed the emotions around in his head since the day he pulled her out of the cell in that hive. Yes, he loved her, but he had promised himself one thing above all else. If it came to this moment, he would never let it get as far as it had with his brother. He hadn't been strong enough. The knowledge his brother had her now sickened him. Marty's cheeks burned. Sticky sweat lined the palms of his hands, eager for his sword. He very much wanted to take Ron's head for relaying the message.

"You tell that goddamn Jake monster to fuck the hell off!" Globs of spittle carried Ike's words to their intruder.

Marty concurred the sentiment with a stern nod.

"Monster?" Ron asked.

They both regarded the man in disbelief. Jake was a monster, but it was probable anyone networked in would see him in some other light.

Bento had settled some, sitting in the tall grass watching them. The dog hadn't made a noise since the man first startled the dog. Only that yapping and yelping seemed to affect the network, allow someone to be free of Jake's command. Yet this guy seemed to have his own thoughts on the matter.

Can someone be networked in, yet live as they please?

He tried to play out the scenarios, deciding on the validity of each.

After a long moment, Ron said, "Our master requests your presence."

"Master? What the fuck did you call him *master* for?"

Ron eyed Ike with peculiar sympathy, as if Ike should have known all along. "Our savior came back to take us home."

Marty had heard those words once before. Those words had haunted him for a very long time. He knew this day would come. Now, here it was, already questioning his sanity.

"Tell Jake we will see him when we see him." Marty eased his hands and let them fall to his sides.

Marty spun away in disgust, having nothing more to discuss with the man. As if realizing this, Ron started back down the hill.

"He said he would wait for you at Bernard's," Ron said.

"Well, tell that fucko we will fuck his shit up when we get there, little Ronnie," Ike said, throwing his balled-up fists into the air. "You bastard son of a cock."

Now that's the Ike I remember.

"Well, guess we know for sure now, don't we?" Ike said as he ran up beside Marty.

Marty studied him, trying to decipher his willingness to go on such an important journey. Ike had plenty of anger, but did he want to end this enough to risk everything? Because risk was what this was all about. Marty had gambled much, put it all out on the table. Especially, if that brought an end to things between his brother and him. His only worry was the same it always had been, that Jake always seemed to be one step ahead of him. That was the primary reason Jake was always so successful at those childhood games they played. He would succumb to losing a battle if that meant he won the war. Jake was a great strategist, and Marty likened himself to more of a thinker. Sometimes he even over-thought matters. He believed what Jake required of Marty was confirmation, proof of his superiority over his brother.

"Yes," Marty finally said.

"This is going to suck ass, my old friend."

"I know." Marty threw an arm over Ike's shoulder and thought well of the man. "It's good to have you here beside me at a time like this. It's good to have a true brother."

Ike's face flushed, and a single tear welled in his eye. He

tried to hide the fact, but it was too late.

Marty smiled.

"Ah, shut up, fucker." Ike shoved Marty away in jest. He mocked as though he would punch Marty, and the two of them laughed off the uncomfortable moment. "Come on, Becca's got some food for us to take with."

Marty smiled. "That's good, because I doubt anyone could live off your cooking."

Chapter 15

The Infinite sat at the table scanning his network best he could, trying to ignore the interference. With his plan now set in motion, he was having difficulty determining how matters were progressing. He wondered if Sheila would arrive soon. He believed she would. He considered Bernard. Perhaps his grasp on the man hadn't been as strong as he recalled. Yet, it should be impossible for any human to deny the Infinite's power.

A woman came to the door. She remained in the entryway for a moment, then rushed over to the table and placed a loaf of bread on it. The Infinite had no use for such foods, so he waved a hand to dismiss her. The thought of eating the bread sickened him.

She went to leave, and he called out to her. "Don't forget this, my dear."

The woman came forward, took the bread, and scurried out through the door. Before she went out of view, she turned and regarded him with sorrow-filled eyes.

The Infinite enjoyed this sentiment very much.

"I'm sorry I disappoint, Lord," Tia said.

Oh yes, the groveling was a nice touch. The Infinite could get used to these praises. So far, his plan had gone well. Soon, he would need to start a rebellion, as he no longer required what help the aliens could provide. He would have everything he wanted, including their ship now that he had bred an entire race to help him secure it. After working out the finer details, he would have Marty, too.

The Infinite considered the bigger picture, his plans

unfolding within his thoughts. After this, he would look to conquer other worlds, some a great distance from here. His new race would exist on different levels, all of them created in the image of their maker, the Infinite. By his side, through it all, would be his brother Marty. No, not Marty. His brother would need a different name if he was to serve next to the Infinite. Marty needed to die, and he would be reborn as one of them. Together, his brother and he would rule the galaxies. The Infinite had been born for this very task.

Tia left, closing the door with care, and for a moment the Infinite was alone. He enjoyed times like this, but perhaps not as much as he did the people worshipping him.

Jake's memories were instrumental in establishing a convincing ruse. Even then, human beings were so gullible. Many would accept who he appeared to be without him having to perform another miracle to convince them. Those who had been present when he healed Dave would talk to those who hadn't been in attendance. They would help form the bridge between the Infinite and anyone who remained skeptical. Eventually, every one of them would accept the Infinite as the second coming of Christ. The fact such a phenomenon should occur so soon after the recent apocalypse made sense and would only reinforce that concept for these hopeless meat bags. Though he despised that human side of himself, Jake's knowledge had been helpful.

The Infinite considered Christianity, trying to decide which details he needed to be accurate with and which he might bend. Already, the sight of his neck wound had been a sticky point to a few humans, thanks to his brother. But these people had never met Jesus, so they couldn't possibly know what Christ looked like any more than Jake did. The Infinite would use this to his advantage and lie, for dishonesty gotten him this far.

He examined his robe, fashioned out of a tablecloth. It would be more convincing if it had been white instead of light blue. Almost all images of Jesus throughout Jake's memories portrayed a mystic man in white linens. The Infinite worried this might also hinder the course of acceptance, but it hadn't. That made him smile, thinking it silly to worry about such trivial matters when he could always resort to force should the need arise.

Someone knocked, then opened the door.

"Sheila?" This overwhelmed the Infinite with delight. "So nice to see you again, under better circumstances, mind you."

She only stared at him, disturbed by what she was seeing, but unable to fight it. On the inside, she might feel distraught, be crying out for Marty even, but no one could hear her.

The Infinite searched her thoughts and feelings, confirming this, but he glimpsed something else, too. She was hiding something, and yet he could not identify what. That was all thanks to the frustrating static that continuously filled the network. As long as that remained, he could discover little.

"What shall I do?" she asked.

The Infinite considered his power over the woman. He could kill her now, and in some ways, he wanted to. The Infinite was jealous of Marty having *this* over him. He could force her to kill herself.

No!

That came from Jake, who also had muddled through those conflicted emotions. Jake wouldn't want him to kill her. Jake would rather fester away in the jealousy eternally than sacrifice his brother's love interest. Jake wouldn't have to do anything. When the time came, the Infinite would decide how best to handle this woman, and he would resolve the matter it for Jake. But not just yet.

"Tia," the Infinite said.

Though he doubted she could hear him calling her through even the thin walls of the shanty, the frightened woman appeared behind Sheila, looking eager to please.

"My friend Sheila requires rest. Will you find her someplace to be alone for a while?"

Tia twiddled her thumbs, overwhelmed by his beauty and what he represented. "Yes, Master…yes. Absolutely."

"Rest now, Sheila. You've traveled far. We can talk more later."

The Infinite would talk to her once the static faded. Then, he would uncover Sheila's secret. He would use it as leverage against Marty, to break his brother. This time Marty would be by his side whether or not he liked it.

"Now leave," the Infinite said. "The both of you."

The women obeyed his wishes, and, for a moment, he had time to himself again. He searched the network, trying to find out what he wanted to know, but still could see nothing.

"Sir?" A man appeared at the door. He was carrying some meat.

The Infinite despised their necessity for food. He despised their meat more than anything. He waved his hand, dismissing the man.

A frown formed on the man's face, knowing he hadn't appeased his Lord Almighty.

Oh well, the Infinite's will be done.

He laughed out loud regarding the blasphemy he now fully submersed himself in.

Chapter 16

N^{ow.} Sandy blinked her eyes.

Now. Now.

She let a smile curl at the corner of her mouth.

Now. Now. Now.

This was the one word she had used to torture Marty's brother. Sandy couldn't put all her attention to it, but she focused on it enough to maintain an echo of the word, so it disrupted the network. That would make it difficult to hear anything. She could sense the way it tortured the monster, the way it reminded Jake of the battle he had lost. And that made her want to laugh.

Now.

Not only this, but she could see how her effort affected Bernard. She didn't fully trust him after all these years. Why? Because when it came down to it, lugs like Bernard weren't strong enough mentally to bypass suggestion. At the moment, Jake was no doubt pushing some disastrous thought to Bernard. She could detect Bernard trying to search for that suggestion, maybe even wanting to hear it.

Now. Now.

Sandy couldn't let her guard down. She knew this from the moment she found herself trapped on the ship, after the battle. Much time passed, but her resolve always remained the same. The mission, although tweaked in small ways, was the same as it always was. Sandy would not surrender. She would see the job through, and she fully planned to stop Jake again. For now, this was all she could do.

The word reminded her of something—more so, of someone. She wondered how Ike had faired, realizing she hadn't bothered to ask. It wasn't so much she had an interest in him, but she had a special respect for the weasel. He had a way of knowing things, but the means in which he obtained his knowledge was crude.

Now. Now.

Bernard looked at Sandy, as if attempting to search her thoughts. His expression displayed his frustration in uncovering nothing of importance. He turned an ear to the sky, perhaps trying to tune in the voice he longed to hear. Sandy thought she knew what would happen if he ever tuned that voice in.

Now.

She sensed the creature not too far away, eager to put an end to this troublesome interference. She liked the fact her efforts frustrated Jake. An angered foe made for a weakened foe. Some people—and from what Sandy gathered of the aliens, too—spent so much time battling the demons within that they often neglected the war on the outside. This was how Sandy planned to defeat Jake. But she would need help, Marty and Ike, too.

Now. Now. Now. Now.

The word had become annoying to even her at some point. She could no longer recall when that moment came, only that it had, long ago. Over time, the ability to reverberate the word through the network had almost become too easy for her, though—second nature. Still, she didn't dare let her guard down for fear someone would break her focus, although she wasn't certain if even that would sever her broadcast at this point.

Now. Now.

She looked down at her horse. Its long legs strode slow upon the grass. Nancy rode a smaller horse. Bernard walked behind them. His mind kept busy, and Sandy thought for sure Nancy noticed his preoccupation. Nancy's face was a varied array of emotions.

As Sandy reflected on their trouble-filled love, she let the one guilty pleasure of her own life creep back inside. With his memory, she drifted back in her recollections, and a flood of guilt washed over her.

Now.

"Stop it, Greg," she said.

He slid his hand up from her butt to the small of her back.

"That won't do either, and you know it."

"Sorry."

He swung his hand behind his back and followed close behind her as they made their way down the tunnel. At the end of the corridor, they came to a large conference room. Standard aluminum folding chairs lined the floor, thirteen in total. Some attendees were already present. Others were still on their way. Standing beside a podium at the front of the room was the Dr. Xavier Deradis.

Sandy watched as the doctor sorted papers with nervous hands, not acknowledging their entrance. When he finally did, he looked surprised as he observed them through his thick-rimmed glasses.

"Masterson." The doctor nodded at Sandy. "Cooley." Again, he nodded. Both received the gesture and snapped their hands to their bills in unison, clicking their heels together as they saluted the good doctor.

"Relax, you two." The doctor adjusted the tightness of his collar. "There is no need for such formalities for me."

They did. She let her arms drop to her sides and folded her hands behind her. Greg did the same, but Sandy thought she felt Greg's hand brush against her ass when he did. She liked his hands. How rough they were and felt. The fact he had all those calluses spoke of the man he was. She liked his steel-colored eyes. His coarse abs rippled with muscles so few men could maintain. Both his biceps and triceps bulged out on his thick arms. A tuft of thick, black hair sat atop the high and tight cut on his head. He had an ass to die for. Right then, standing in front of the doctor, desire stirred deep within her. She struggled to drive the thought of a nude Greg out of her mind and cleared her throat.

Greg looked over at her and smiled. She didn't return the favor.

"So," the doctor said, and turned back to his paperwork, "Take your seats, lovebirds."

Panic struck Sandy. Her heart pumped fast, ready to implode in her chest. She felt her hands tremble. Sweat formed on her brow, and she wondered if Cooley felt likewise. She didn't dare look at him for fear of proving the doctor right.

The doctor looked surprised. "What? I'm kidding, you two. Now, take your seats already."

They found two folding chairs of shoddy construction in the back, the sort one paid less than a couple bucks for at any general goods store across America—through she suspected the government paid top dollar for to some foreign country. As they sat, a few stragglers entered from the corridor. The doctor greeted each in the same awkward manner. When all were ready, the doctor started the briefing.

Over three hours later, the doctor finished and asked if there were questions. There wouldn't be. All of them understood their job. This wasn't the Army, the Marines, Air Force, or any other incarnation of the men who served this country. This was something different—a group without a title in the government. They referred to themselves as the Unlucky Thirteen. It was a fitting moniker, considering what they had gone up against before and what they were about to go up against.

"Masterson, you'll be first," the doctor said.

Her heart fluttered upon hearing her name. She wanted to take Greg's hand. Of course, they would pick the woman. Women were expendable, weren't they? Or was it a simple "women first" courtesy in this case? The sourness in her gut was difficult to deny. It felt like she was on a roller coaster, rising toward that big decline, about to go over the crest and rush downward.

Greg glanced her way.

She realized she was letting on too much but didn't think anyone could discern this about her behavior. Greg knew her too well. She opened her mouth to confirm that she had heard the doctor's orders, when Greg stood and snapped his heels together. He folded his hands behind his back. He made a gesture only a few could see, Sandy included. She heard them cough and grunt quiet laughter as Greg extended his middle finger to her.

What is he doing?

"Sir?" Greg said.

"Yes, Cooley. You can dispense with all the formal lingo."

Even though the doctor kept reminding them of this, it broke none of them of the habit.

"I'd like to go first if I may." Greg looked down at her.

Sandy wanted to stop him. She wanted to make a point she was perfectly capable of serving her country, and she would do her job well. All she had to do was stand and insist upon it. She knew what this meant. Screw the whole women first tradition— all these men would follow Greg's lead, either out of chivalrous pity or to show they were as good a man as he was. All she had to do was object.

Only she didn't.

"All right, all right, Cooley. If you must."

Greg shot a hint of a smile at Sandy. "Oh, I must."

Sandy was both thankful for and resented the gesture. One by one, the others took their places in a line before her, and she found herself somehow stuck at the end, no longer a need to even offer her services.

So, chivalry is not dead.

Later, she would thank Greg. She would never say it, of course, but she would give him pleasures he had only dreamed about. With that thought popping in her mind, the stirring sensation worked its way back to her. This time she wasn't so quick to dismiss it.

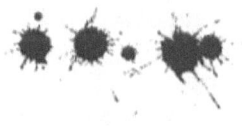

"Sandy," Nancy said, "Did you say something, dear?"

The interruption shook her back to the present. Sandy gazed at Nancy's patient face, seeing that she was waiting for an answer. Sandy tossed the question around in her head until it made sense. When it finally did, she couldn't help but look at Bernard.

She answered with a shake of her head.

"Funny, I could have sworn I saw your lips moving."

Sandy doubted she would have done that, but perhaps she had. She had been alone for so long. Who knew what one did amid daydreaming after what she had been through?

Now.

Bernard's eyes probed her. She knew what he was looking for. Before long, he would figure it out. No way she could keep this game up forever, but her intention was to continue it for as long as she could manage. With any luck, that would be long enough for Marty to kill Jake for good this time.

The stymied look in Bernard's eyes suggested she had succeeded.

What concerned Sandy was that she had lost a step. Not because she could no longer take down a man of Bernard's size, but because she had lost a lot of weight on the ship, and, with it, she had lost a lot of strength. It was more than a physical loss, though. Sandy knew she wasn't right in the head—not that she was altogether there to begin with. She had already been on edge long before her stint on the ship. Living alone for so long with no one else had just sealed that fate. It was just like being stranded on a desolate island which made her a castaway, returned home and told to just pick up right where she left off.

Now. Now.

What if Bernard found out what she was doing? What would he do? She didn't think he would sacrifice his relationship with Nancy.

Or would he? Hadn't he been on the fringe of this decision once before? What had been his choice then?

Now.

If he decided it would be best to do something about her interference, Sandy would have no choice but to fight. She thought she was ready and had even prepared as much as she could. How would Nancy react if it came to that? Sandy had lost the woman's trust long ago, so would she try to stop Sandy?

Did Sandy have it in her to stop both Bernard and Nancy? She wasn't sure.

For now, she let her mind drift back to Greg a little longer.

As she let herself sink back into her past, Bernard stared at her with an intense look in his eyes. He was probing her mind even then. Nancy was oblivious to this virtual back and forth, but Sandy believed the woman would never fully trust her again. Sandy had killed Bernard right before Nancy's eyes. And she would do it again if she needed to.

Now.

Chapter 17

"Now, now, hot stuff."

Sandy shoved him against the wall and reached around him to open the door. He leaned in and kissed her. She couldn't help but feel a little paranoid about kissing out in the open but allowed it. Afterward, she spun him in front of her and placed her hand in the small of his back, urging him to get going.

She grinned. "Come on, let's go."

Thinking better of it, Sandy took his hand anyway and led him down the corridor. There was no time left for discussion despite her doubts. As they neared the lab, she let her hand drop from his. He tried to take it back, but she shook him off.

"Greg," she said, her tone backing up her stance on the matter. "We can't."

"Come on, Sandy, one more—" Before he could finish the sentence, their sergeant came from around the corner.

"One more what, Corporal?"

The man's broad chest blocked their path, a sign he fully expected an answer. The way he kept his peppered hair trimmed short, reminded Sandy of a beach she visited as a kid— the only time in her life she had seen such a place. Those deep-set black eyes examined them, his expression revealing the fact he thought them both worthless. To him, they were expendable at the very least.

"Nothing, Sir." Sandy answered with a click of her heels and a standard salute.

She nudged Cooley, trying to avoid being seen. He followed

her lead and snapped off a hard salute. It was sometimes difficult in this place to remember who to salute and who not to with so many of the non-military personnel in this underground facility not caring for the gesture. That alone made soldiers lazy, so they all saluted everyone, anyway.

"I see." His eyes studied them. As if satisfied all was well, he moved on with his conversation. "Good luck in there, Cooley."

"Yes, Sir. Looking forward to it."

"Well, off with you then." The sergeant brushed alongside them to pass, carefully studying their closeness, perhaps seeing something. But maybe he hadn't. Could it be that he wasn't even looking for anything in particular? Surely, he must have some notion what was going on between Cooley and her.

A man like him always has reasons for prying.

They rushed toward the medical lab, both hugging the wall. When the sergeant was out of sight, Greg leaned back and gave Sandy a quick peck on her cheek. It could be the last kiss she ever received from his lips, so she cherished the moment and how it surprised her.

"Ah, Cooley," the doctor said, acknowledging his approach. "So, are we ready?"

Greg went to salute but didn't. He shook the doctor's hand instead.

Sandy stood rigid. "Doctor."

"Greetings, Masterson."

"Okay, Cooley, let's get started, shall we?"

"It's your dime, doc."

Sandy scanned the room and saw the other eleven soldiers lined up along the walls. There wasn't much room for anyone else. All of them focused on the doctor as he led Greg to a chair and began strapping him down. Sandy took a spot with the rest of her team.

A thought popped into her head. *What could this really lead to?*

She could lose Greg forever. Sure, there was always that possibility in a profession like theirs. Hadn't the doctor explained how different this would be? There was also a need for trust on all parts. And they both trusted their government, and they even trusted the odd-looking doctor with his thick-rimmed glasses.

Sandy couldn't help comparing the chair Greg sat in to an electric chair, positioned inside a jail-like room that stemmed off from the medical lab. There were several other barred off rooms, all with the same standard methods of protection. Here, Greg would remain until they determined whether the test had been a success. Sandy's confirmed her worst fears when a small metal cap came down upon a wet sponge atop Greg's head. They fully intended to kill him if things went haywire.

The doctor placed a black rubber wedge in Greg's mouth.

Panic struck her when she identified, for the first time, the soldier by the switch. He was there in case things went bad, but right then she wanted to replace Greg. More so, she desired to profess her love for him right here out in the open. She had to stop this from happening, but she couldn't. This was their job, so she had no choice but to sit tight and watch along with all the other soldiers.

Thoughts of their last kiss ran through her head. How sweet it had been. So innocent yet forbidden. She considered the softness of the kiss, how the scruff on his upper lip had tickled her left cheek. Her legs had trembled then, and she had needed to take a to calm her nerves more than anything. Just thinking of the moment, her heart pattered louder and louder, and she realized she didn't care who saw how emotional she got. She wore her feelings on her sleeve for all to view.

The doctor approached Greg holding something in his hands. Greg waited, eager to serve his country. When the doctor was close enough, he removed the protective plastic from the needle and held it in front of Greg. Menacing in size, he didn't hesitate to stick Greg's arm before stepping away. Everyone watched in anticipation of what came next.

Nothing happened for a long time.

"Okay," the doctor said. "Let's see how it takes to you, Cooley."

That's it? All this for a fucking shot in the arm?

Relief washed over her, and, for a moment, all was well. She remained damp with perspiration. Her fingers still twitched, and her vision was fuzzy, much the result of all this self-induced stress. As all the feelings began to subside, it reminded her of exiting a swimming pool—how she would feel wet and cool. But the feeling didn't last long.

Greg shuddered against his restraints. The doctor only stood there, taking notes, not a single look of surprise upon his face. Right then, it looked as though the electric chair had gone live, with Greg rocking left and then right so hard she wondered if the restraints would hold. His eyes went back in his head, the pain visibly so intense he appeared on the verge of passing out. Foamy spittle formed in the corners of his mouth, around the rubber wedge pinched between his teeth. The veins in his muscles rippled as he tried to lift himself out of the seat.

Sandy had the sudden urge to jump out of her chair. Her eyes trained on the soldier standing near the switches. All of this resulted from whatever poisons the doctor had injected into Greg's bloodstream. As her panic heightened, Greg finally fell limp.

She watched from the edge of her seat as the doctor removed the black rubber from his mouth and wiped away the saliva. Greg took a deep breath and sank into the stiff chair, letting his arms and legs dangle loosely within their respective restraints. When he exhaled, his breath was unhindered and easy.

Oddly, though, he looked different somehow. Maybe more handsome. The restraints and metal cap of death remained attached to Greg, but when his eyes found her, his already mesmerizing gaze stunned her. Sandy wanted to run to him, but she stayed put.

Another scientist approached and examined Greg. He looked at the doctor with a sly expression, his eyes thinning to small slits. "It's begun."

The doctor's eyes widened, but Sandy's heart sank.

Chapter 18

Marty and Ike set off across the valley to find Bernard. There was strength in numbers, no matter how old and worn they were now. To Ike, their odds were even better with this *new* Marty. He wasn't the man caught in turmoil over having a leadership role anymore. Ike wondered where a man might find that level of confidence. Marty even rode his horse straight and proper, perhaps taught to ride that way. Or maybe Marty had grown some on the inside, and maybe that helped him walk a little taller, too.

No one ever taught Ike how to ride a horse, so he sat hunched forward, holding on for dear life. There had been only a few words spoken between them over the many miles since they left Becca. Ike had many questions twirling around in his head, but he thought he could develop his own answers for most of them. For instance, were they going to die? Ike thought so. But Ike wasn't one for complete quiet, either.

"What'cha thinking on, Marty?" Ike said, wanting to break the silence.

Marty shook his head, considering everything. "Nothing," he said, not speaking of whatever it might be.

"Come on, brother. Share with yer good 'ole buddy." He smiled and winked at Marty.

Marty looked down at Bento. That little shit of a dog never left by his side. Bento couldn't be more than three years old. Most domesticated animals were either feral or destroyed, or worse yet, eaten. No one Ike knew—other than Marty, that was— kept a pet anymore.

"I was thinking about Bento," Marty said.

"Hmm, all this going on—us heading to our likely death, and you're daydreaming about a freaking dog?"

Marty chuckled but nodded.

"I don't get it. What's so special about this damn dog, anyway?"

"Nothing, maybe." Marty offered a sullen look to Ike. "But, maybe, he might have some special role to play in all this."

"A role? What fucking role, Marty? He's a frigging nut-licking mutt."

"I'm not sure. Maybe he doesn't."

"Then why did you get the goddamn thing?"

Marty went to answer but stopped. Then he said, "He sort of found me."

Ike didn't press him any further. It was clear there was more to this dog than Ike could fathom. What? He did not know. Whatever the case, Marty slipped back into silence, back to thinking about Bento, perhaps how they met.

Chapter 19

M arty thought back to that day.

He never really had been a city boy, but it was sad to see they had all gone south in such a short time. The streets were still wet from an early morning dousing of rain. A strange, smoldering smoke rose from one building, so Marty steered clear in case it was a group of pillagers. For the last several weeks, Marty had kept his eye out for animals. No one else paid them much attention, except for maybe livestock, but Marty watched the other animals. Specifically, he looked for the dogs, mostly because he had a hunch.

At first, he wasn't sure why. A small part of him wished for some additional companionship beyond what Sheila could provide, but that wasn't the real reason. There was something odd about the way people had abandoned their pets. Perhaps they no longer trusted such creatures. Marty himself had been leery of eating anything produced from farm animals at first, for fear of them being infected. Plus, any animal was an additional mouth to feed, and while food no longer cost money, it was becoming more and more difficult to provide enough for the whole table.

What Marty saw was something more than the removal of such distinct relationships out of need alone. These animals were avoiding humans. Even the most secure of places should expect to see a feral dog or cat come to beg for scraps. But they didn't, which led to Marty's investigation. Then, one day, he found some of them.

Three dogs and two cats entered a barn which lay in

shambles. Marty hid and observed. Another dog and two cats followed. One dog popped his head back out, looked in Marty's direction. He didn't think the dog saw him, but even if it had, it wouldn't have deemed Marty a worthy opponent. That became clear when the dog disappeared back into the barn.

Marty stood, and, taking careful steps, approached the barn while keeping an eye out for any other dogs or cats. When Marty got close enough, he got down and crept the rest of the way to the barn entrance on all fours. He couldn't get there fast enough and wanted desperately to get up and scurry over, but he didn't, refusing to let his emotions rule the moment. It had taken a while to find them, and he didn't want to scare them off.

He reached to his hip and readied the rope he had fastened there. Marty had been practicing his roping skills for months now. He would need to be quick and accurate if he meant to capture one. As he neared the door, a growling muzzle stared him down.

The mangy mutt's breath wreaked of stale odor. Despite how skinny the dog was, Marty thought the odds were still well within the animal's favor, Should Marty try, he would not escape unscathed. He might get his sword in time to kill the dog, but he didn't want to. Plus, he was sure the action would lead to a much larger attack.

The dog's lips drew back, quivering over sharp teeth. It growled again, quieter this time, the dog's focus never breaking. The dog's feet shifted forward mere millimeters in response a movement from Marty. Its entire body lurched forward, as if to show its intentions. But the dog stayed back.

Sweat beaded on Marty's forehead. He wanted to swipe it away but worried the dog see that as a threat. Instead, it dripped down into his eyes, stinging them. Marty blinked, trying to relieve them, but as this need to wipe away the sweat intensified, so did the dog's visible anger.

Now Marty turned his attention to his sword. He thought the dog might hurt him if it got hold of his arm. Could he kill the dog before it got to him? While pondering his move, another dog came and stood beside the first. This dog was a dark brown Lab, its gaze wiser but sorrowful. This dog didn't growl or even sneer, so it posed no threat to Marty. The Lab's eyes searched Marty, as if searching for something. Then, it turned to the growling dog and stared at it until the mangy dog stopped growling. A second later, that dog went inside, leaving Marty with the very dog he hoped to rope.

Thoughts raced through Marty's mind.

Can I rope the dog from this close?

Would he even need to?

Most of his thoughts revolved around what this dog might be, what threat it posed to humanity, and how it had gotten this way. Marty stared into the dog's large brown eyes. Somehow, it seemed to understand his quandary. The dog shifted forward and sniffed Marty, perhaps detecting something from long ago that no human could detect. Marty imagined the stench might not be a good one, or, at least, he hoped that was the case. That this dog despised that old smell.

The dog inched closer, letting its paws come within inches of Marty. Marty considered the rope, then let it pass. The dog came even closer until Marty began to worry what it might do to him. Then, suddenly, Marty felt something unusual.

An image darted into his mind. It was that of a chocolate lab appearing as if lightning had struck it. Yet, there had been no visible lightning. This invisible bolt of energy passed through the dog, and Marty recognized this as what his brother had endured before he became a monster. Somehow this dog remained unaffected in the same way. Yet, it had undergone some transformation. It seemed more *intelligent*, strong enough to push a vision to Marty. And that was precisely what had interested Marty regarding the dog, that he could potentially use the dog as an early warning system.

Chapter 20

B ernard pushed but nothing went through. He studied Sandy, who appeared engrossed with her own thoughts. She was so much stronger now. Was she blocking him? He knew she had revitalized fast thanks to Nancy's aid, but he had expected she would need time to recover. But she was good as new already, and that was something he hadn't foreseen.

There was something more to her ability now, too. He could sense her strength. She had created a mental obstruction that prevented him from getting what he wanted most, to hear the network. To hear the words, which instead were being overridden by an endless static. Bernard wanted to hear those other voices with clarity.

No, he *needed* to hear those words.

He was certain that upon hearing them he would discern for himself whether he could trust them. But hear them he would, eventually. It was his frustration in not hearing those voices that got him started trying to push words to Sandy. He aimed them at her deliberately, trying to pry open whatever door she had slammed shut between them. Earlier, she had given him a peek behind that barrier, but had since closed him off. Why, he couldn't be sure, but he would get in.

I will kill you, he pushed, but she didn't appear to hear this thought.

He felt somewhat guilt for pushing such an angry message, but in another, more selfish way, it was liberating. She had already killed him once before.

She deserves a dose of her own medicine.

Bernard wondered if given the opportunity if he could kill her.

His eyes searched Nancy. He adored her. But there were more important concerns right now. He couldn't bother with love or the consequences of what he was thinking. That was all part of discovering his own path for himself. First, he needed this other part of him to get stronger, because that part of him belonged. Being torn emotionally like this, angered him. Because of that anger, he couldn't help but leer at Sandy with defiance.

I will kill you.

She remained unmoved by his words. Bernard thought she even looked calmer than ever, drifting along on her horse as if she were about to fall sleep. She wore Nancy's clothes as if they were her own. That alone somehow dirtied them for him.

Does that make Nancy wrong, too? For helping her?

Bernard found Nancy's eyes. She peered back at him with adoration. It was a sentiment he wanted to share, as those moments had been few and far apart these days. He wanted to stay with Nancy. But it was all so much more complicated than that.

He forced a smile to his lips, knowing it would look out of place. She smiled back.

What does she think about all this?

Did she question what he had gone through? What he had become? What sorts of things he might still become?

Anger festered inside him, too. He gazed at Sandy with such vitriol that a vile taste formed in his mouth.

I will kill you.

When he pushed this thought, he imagined committing the act. He thrust a knife into the woman's stomach and stood back, watching her bleed out. Still, there was no response. But he couldn't help but grin.

"We should stop here for the night," he said, mindlessly.

The horses stopped side by side, the women on top of them looked back at him with clear doubt. There was still plenty of daylight left.

"We should keep going," Sandy said. "There won't be much time."

"Bernard knows what's best," Nancy said.

Sandy looked at her and grinned. It didn't appear genuine. It expressed a troubled woman who conceded, even if it sounded silly and dangerous to her. And Bernard knew why Sandy thought it a mistake, too.

She hears me.

Nancy jumped down from her horse and started unpacking. Bernard helped her, and they worked fast to set up camp. A reluctant Sandy remained on her horse, watching the two of them. Bernard ignored her, focusing on their bedding.

After a few minutes, Sandy dismounted. Bernard watched her feet hit the ground and observed the muscles in her legs. They had weakened a lot over the last year, but their power had returned to a large degree. Soon, he might not be able to take her down if he had to. Bernard wasn't smart enough to create opportunities, but he often relied on brute strength in a fight, as he was a bigger man. That and he wasn't sure he could bring himself to shoot her even if she had shot him first.

Nancy pulled a small shovel from her pack, making clear her intention of needing to go to the bathroom. Before Nancy left, Bernard tried once more.

I will kill you.

Chapter 21

"What did you say?" Sandy asked Bernard. Nancy searched Sandy, trying to decipher what had alarmed her, because that had come through in her tone. But Sandy didn't stop eyeing up Bernard, even going so far to let an accusing smirk show on her face.

Bernard just stared at her, his surprise matching Nancy's.

"What the fuck did you say, Bernard?" Sandy stood defiantly and moved closer to the man.

Still, Bernard didn't answer.

"Sandy, please." Nancy wanted to diffuse the situation, but Sandy didn't seem interested.

A troublesome glare appeared in Sandy's eyes. In her thoughts, Nancy saw Sandy holding the gun, the barrel aimed at Bernard, with Sandy about to pull the trigger. No matter how close they got, those images would always haunt Nancy's thoughts. There was no changing the past.

"You said you would kill me," Sandy said to Bernard, glancing to Nancy. "He said he wanted to kill me, Nancy."

Sandy seemed to hope Nancy had heard this. But Nancy had noticed nothing but the crazed look in Sandy's eyes. The woman was crazy—had been for some time.

Makes sense she would think Bernard was trying to kill her, Nancy rationalized.

Bernard shrugged when Nancy's eyes fell upon him. Confusion overwhelmed her what was transpiring, what had taken place already between the two that she could never know about. It was difficult to keep all those old images out of her head, the anger and resentment she had because of what Sandy had done suppressed. Her hands tightened around the handle of the small shovel in her hands.

"Why would you say such a thing, Bernard?" Sandy shouted this time. Her voice echoed across the land, bouncing back off the few war-torn buildings and houses.

Bernard still didn't answer.

Sandy moved closer, standing in front of her now. Nancy couldn't be sure if she did this to keep her from intervening or to protect her from Bernard.

In her head, Nancy saw the smoke, the blood, Bernard falling to the ground in pain. The anger boiled inside her, still waiting to erupt after all this time.

Sandy stabbed a finger at Bernard.

He cowered away.

Sandy took another step toward him.

Nancy followed, staying close behind Sandy. She saw things escalating. This was getting out of control. Most of all, she couldn't keep that image of the gun from forming in Sandy's hands, even though she knew there wasn't one there. The gun was in Nancy's pack.

Or is it?

Bernard patted the air and said, "Sandy, I don't know—"

He never got the chance to finish. A pinging sound filled Nancy's ears. She stood above Sandy's collapsing body with the shovel gripped in both hands. Below her, a rush of red covered Sandy's head, matching the blood on the shovel.

Nancy didn't think Sandy dead. If she was, then so be it. The woman had it coming for what she did to Bernard. Dead or not, Sandy would never get the chance to commit that crime again. Not as long as Nancy had breath in her lungs.

Chapter 22

Marty laid a thin blanket on the ground. They wouldn't have much time to sleep, but a little rest would do them and the horses good. He observed Ike putting down his own bedding, piling up a wad of clothes for his head.

Ike saw this and grinned. "What the fuck you looking at?"

Marty couldn't help but laugh. "Nothing, my old friend."

Ike turned and sat on the clothes, reaching back for his pack with that coy smile still on his face. He held a small metal flask, shaking it Marty's direction. "Hair of the dog's ass that done killed you?"

Marty shook it off. He needed to keep a clear head. Besides, he never had been much of a drinker.

Ike stared at the flask, as if daring himself to take a drink by his lonesome. It was as if something inside of Ike prevented him from drinking alone. He replaced the flask in his pack with reluctance and gazed up at the night sky. Marty thought Ike had many questions, and his old friend always had his doubts. He was unsure if he could resolve anything for Ike, though, as Marty still had his own qualms. It was highly doubtful Sheila was still back at their farm, safe from everything.

Try not to think about her.

That was easier said than done.

Ike struggled to get something out, choosing not to say anything.

"What?" Marty asked.

"Well, it's just so fucking stupid, you know?" Ike's face flushed orange thanks to the campfire. He stared long and hard into Marty's eyes. "But do you think we will die, Marty?"

It honored Marty that a man like Ike could ask him this question. He considered it with careful thought and remembered Bernard had asked him the same thing when last time their lives were in such a delicate imbalance. His answer back then hadn't really been an answer at all. His choice had been not to feed the doubt. This was different. Times had changed. And something inside of Marty knew Ike needed the straight and narrow.

"I think there's a good chance."

Ike's eyes trailed off toward his home, perhaps attempting to hold back some emotion. He reached back into the pack and took a firm hold on the flask. Without hesitation, Ike unscrewed the cap and lifted it to his lips with a slight toasting gesture in Marty's direction. Marty watched Ike take three solid tugs off the flask.

"What the fuck, eh?" Ike said.

Marty smiled, held out a hand for the flask. Ike passed it over, and Marty raised the flask to his own lips, toasting Ike and the napping Bento. He took a deep swallow.

Scotch—a good blend, too. It went down easy, leaving a hot trail of warmth in Marty's throat as it sank into his belly. There, it heated the rest of his body like a radiant sun.

"What the fuck, indeed." Marty passed the flask back to Ike. As he did, a warm flush crossed his cheeks at the embarrassment of speaking such a bold curse.

This made Ike laugh. He took another drink, and the two men passed the flask back and forth until they finished the scotch, without another word passing between them.

Chapter 23

His eyes opened wide as he sat up in the chair from a slinking posture. The woman washing his feet looked up at him with surprise. Finding her, he dismissed her out of the room with a wave of his hand and waited until she left.

Hurry, the Infinite thought.

He tracked the woman out through the door. The night sky peeked in right before the rickety door closed. Jake turned an anxious ear to the sky. He could hear it again.

I see you.

The message went out through the network with clarity equal to what it would sound like if he had spoken the words out loud. He could sense them hearing his words. This also pleased the Infinite. As a surge of questions filled the network, he made his presence known and set his plan into motion with one word—the very word that had haunted him for so long.

Now.

Chapter 24

Sandy remembered how it cold was during her time on the ship. How she shivered so often, desperately wanting clothes, but unable to find much. That alone forced her to live like a wild animal in the shadows among her enemies.

Soon after they severed the hive from Earth and brought it onboard, they captured her. They stripped her of her clothes, destroyed them, and then sealed her into one of the hive cells. The hive hadn't had the same effect on Sandy as it did on Bernard, though. They couldn't conduct energy through her the same way they did others, possibly because of the way the good doctor infected her. Once they discovered this, she found herself an actual prisoner; bound, gagged, and caged. Being a prisoner of that nature was actually easier to handle for Sandy, though.

When the opportunity presented itself, Sandy escaped. It hadn't even been that difficult. It was far easier than she had imagined to push a suggestion to her alien captors. So, when Sandy pushed a suggestion for an alien to release her, she immediately had to come up with a means of hiding within the network so they wouldn't find her. What she opted for was a simple mental device she had developed back at the shelter in Illinois. Something constant. A word. Static. She used the same word she had back on Earth, mostly because she was sure it would only anger Marty's brother. Jake hadn't hidden the fact he despised that word, his frustration over what had happened leaking into the network soon after their departure and from then on out, until she started pushing the static. His mind twisted the word around in his thoughts daily, no doubt pondering his failure. But it hadn't been a total failure had it?

Jake got most of what he wanted. He was powerful and in control, whether or not the original aliens knew it. And he had kept most of the hives fully intact. This vast ship would be his castle, able to travel through the universe, pillaging and plundering as he wished. But there was one thing she knew he didn't have. A constant mix of emotions had troubled Jake regarding his brother, Marty.

Sandy had sensed the dismay haunting Jake over not being able to secure his brother. She wasn't sure why Jake needed Marty, or whether his desire might be more of a power trip. She could, however, grasp his sorrow over Marty not being at his side. Over time, it had struck Sandy; he wanted Marty by his side not as an equal but as a sidekick. No, not just a sidekick, but a need to feel superior to Marty. Not only this, but he seemed to require Marty to see this dominance.

When she found the word in Jake's thoughts, she took it and repurposed it. She had been the source of his annoyance. She pushed it, over and over, twirled it around in a sub-network she had created that stemmed off the main one. When she opened the floodgates to the actual network, the word echoed into it as a daunting reminder to Jake. This was the precise trick they had used to keep the network from reaching inside the facility. Back then, they used a machine to provide the static. What she used now was similar but a result of Sandy's trained mind. And it delighted her to further aggravate Jake.

In her dreams, she remembered seeing the thing skitter across her feet. Her eyes darted to the ground, finding a creature that resembled a centipede, except dark blue in coloration. The insect appeared similar to a cockroach, found throughout the ship. And she had been so hungry.

Her hands flashed to the ground to either side of the bug, moving like colliding walls. The bug had hissed at her intrusion, but she ignored the warning. Both hands swiped in and scooped the bug up before it could defend itself. It bit the inside of her left thumb. She ignored the pain. The second bite made it difficult to keep hold of the bug. Its teeth dug into the tender skin of her palm and chewed. She released that hand, squeezing the bug between the fingers of her other hand. Before it could bite her again, she tossed the critter into her mouth.

The bug bit her tongue. The intense pain forced her to all fours as she struggled to get the bug between her teeth. She pushed the bug with her tongue, trying to guide it into position. When she got it there, she immediately brought her teeth down on the bug and felt a crunch. Then a jelly-like substance filled her mouth, tasting like soil. The urge to puke overwhelmed her, but she suppressed the sensation, knowing she had to eat. She had to force the slug-like wad in her mouth down her throat.

Her tongue stung as she swabbed at it with her fingers. The pinchers remained attached, so she yanked them out with a cringe as the flesh of her tongue ripped. A mixture of blood and a strange blue gel coated her fingers, which made for a sticky combination that wouldn't let her throw the pinchers aside. When she finally ridded herself of them, she licked her fingers clean of the gelatin with unsatisfied anxiousness. Her stomach churned, unhappy with her choice of sustenance but doing its best to process the food.

She walked among the shadows of the hives for months to follow, taking what she could when she available, eating the worst of creatures and always cold. But she remained free. Without some weapon or clothes, it had been difficult, but she had succeeded. And now that she was back on her home planet, she felt like the cockroach.

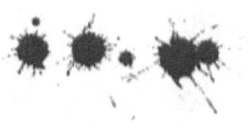

Something cool pressed against her head. A distant ache arose, and she wanted to reach for the tender flesh there. When she did, someone swatted her hand away.

"Hush, let me clean it, Sandy."

The hives shimmered in her memories, fading out of

existence as the present came back into focus. The cloud-filled sky swirled into a fuzzy blanket above her. There, among them she saw Nancy's face.

"Wha...what happened?" Sandy asked.

"Bernard left."

"Did he—"

"No, that was me."

Sandy stared up at the woman, wanting to strangle her. But she also understood why she had done it. Sandy would have done the same in her shoes. The anger subsided quickly, which was good given her current state.

"I'm sorry," Nancy said, sounding like a child who had just received a good scolding.

Sandy waved her off. She sat up, her world spinning and reconstructed Nancy's words.

"Where did he go?" Sandy asked.

Nancy gazed off to where they came from. "Back."

Sandy saw no sign of the big man on the horizon. She wondered how far Nancy followed before coming back for her. Had she even trailed him at all? Perhaps Nancy wasn't so enamored by the man after seeing what he could become. Surely the woman would have tried to entice him to stay at the very least.

"We should go after him." Nancy wore an anxious expression, her need for help obvious. Both knew she couldn't do this alone. She needed Sandy. When Sandy took the compress, Nancy twiddled her thumbs, eager for a response that matched her desire.

"Not yet," Sandy said, pressing the compress against her head. "You really bonked me good. I can't even see straight."

Nancy frowned. Sandy could see the temptation of going on alone in Nancy's eyes as she stared off to where they came from. The woman wasn't as strong as Sandy once thought. She seemed afraid.

"Soon then, maybe after you feel better?" Hope lit Nancy's eyes.

"We need to find Marty."

Nancy stood and huffed away, her arms straight, both fists

balled up at her side. She took a few steps toward where Bernard had gone, as if testing her independence. Sandy could see she wanted to bring Bernard back but doubted she could do it by herself.

"Why Marty?" Nancy asked, staring away from Sandy. "Why do we need anyone else?"

With great effort, Sandy stood and approached Nancy. She still felt woozy from the wallop. At least there was a little fight left in Nancy, even if she had directed it at the wrong person. Sandy laid a hand on Nancy's shoulder, who allowed it. Nancy was crying.

"This isn't about Bernard. It's not about us, either." Sandy shifted her head to meet Nancy's eyes. Doing so made her head throb. "If it were, I would still be back on the ship eating bugs."

"Then who?" Nancy whispered.

"It's about the brothers. We're just caught in the middle."

For a while afterward, the two women lay across from each other without a word passing between them, no fire to warm them. Nancy gazed up at the sky and although Sandy needed it, neither of them could get back to sleep. Even worse, the blow to Sandy's head had left the network undisrupted. Now it was up and running, opening for business. Try as she might, Sandy wasn't able to block it again. Unsure why, she considered it might be because of the large welt on the back of her head. Or maybe whatever Jake had done had grown too strong for her suggestions to disrupt now. Jake had likely been preparing for this moment for a long time.

No worries.

She would try again come morning.

Drifting in and out of sleep, Sandy glimpsed where her dreams were heading. She couldn't help but think of Greg, but not as his human self. She saw him as the monster. No matter how much she struggled against the image, her dreams were going there, and she was too tired to fight it anymore.

Sandy eased her aching head against Bernard's pack, feeling somewhat lucky he left it, and submersed herself in the miseries of her past.

Chapter 25

It was a little after three in the morning when Sandy started down the corridor, taking careful, deliberate steps. Now would be the shift change for the guards, so this was her best chance to visit Greg, though he wouldn't be alone. Smith, Jacobs, Mathers, and Kent had all undergone the procedure already, the timing of each seeming to have little to do with any actual transformation. The rest of the Unlucky Thirteen—her excluded—had died almost immediately after being injected.

Whatever abilities the doctor was trying to get out of these injections, he had been unsuccessful so far. A few of the subjects had begun construction of the desired cells, but the doctor hadn't been able to curate and transfer the technology contained within the cells to a syringe. With her being the lone test subject left, she worried what the doctor planned to do with her. What might she become? Or, not become? She hoped they had run out of ideas, as they kept delaying her injection date. But even if they ran out of ideas, she suspected the injection would eventually go on as planned. There was no way she got out of this unscathed. Knowing that made it difficult to relax.

As she entered the laboratory, a strange glow illuminated the room. The amber hue spread out from Kent's containment room. Kent used a stubby, stinger-like tail to construct a cell. The stinger formed a bulbous tip and squirted a portion of a glue-like substance onto the structure in progress. The creature turned and fine-tuned the liquid into place, smoothing it with its claws. Over and over, the Kent-creature would repeat this process until it finished what the doctor desired.

Greg sat against the wall of his cell, or rather stuck to it, the horrid cocoon all she had left to remember him by. The cocoon trembled, giving her hope that life still existed somewhere inside it. Since arriving, though, the cocoon had not moved one bit.

She found a chair, slid it closer to his room, and sat. Leaning back, she observed the others. A couple were balding, their crimson skin similar to what Greg's had looked like prior to the cocoon. Mathers wasn't as far along. Kent had already gone through the cocoon stage and came out as this monster. Would Greg suffer the same fate?

A piece of the cocoon wavered loose. Seeing this, Sandy leaned forward in the chair and trained her eyes on the small opening. She scooted her butt to the edge using her hands to steady herself and hoped this would turn out well.

"Oh, Greg," she whispered. "Why'd we have to get involved in this?"

"Sandy?"

She thrust herself upright in the chair. The back legs of the chair made an awful sound when she did. She was too afraid to look, certain someone of authority had just joined her in the room. When she dared look, she saw no one.

"You there, Sandy?"

As the voice steadied, she recognized who it had come from—Greg. But she thought it dangerous to expect the man she had fallen in love with to look the same once he came out of that cocoon. Three of the others watched from their rooms—all her old comrades equally curious as to the fate of their fellow soldier. Perhaps they wanted to see what lay in store for them, but they only need look to Kent for that answer.

"Can you help me out of this thing?" Greg asked.

Her eyes retrained on the hole in the cocoon. "Greg?"

"Yes, it's me. Who the heck else would it be?"

She watched the cocoon writhe, as Greg attempted to free himself. There was an urge to help, and she even felt a little anxiety over how he would look. She wanted to free him, to be with him again. Was this her last chance? The two of them could leave this place, put behind the duty they vowed to finish to their death, and start a new life far away from this madness, out of reach of the government. But the additional worry of what Greg might have transformed into soiled her plans.

"Seriously," Greg said, "you want to help me out of this thing or what?"

She went to the keypad for his room and placed her fingertips on it and entered the code. They had made her memorize the code with no knowledge of her history with Cooley, part of her duty being to help contain these men whenever the doctor entered a room. She remained at the keypad, wondering if she could break the rules, wanting to even, but unsure what would come of it.

"Hello? What the hell?" His voice boomed. "You still there, babe?"

What of the man inside that cocoon? Was he already one of *them*? She had no way of knowing, and wouldn't, unless she helped him. Already she had stood by once before and done nothing. Now this opportunity was slipping by.

"Yes," she said, trying to remain quiet, "I'm here."

"Then help me get out of here, will you?"

She typed the code in without even knowing she had done so. The only obstacle that remained was to hit the enter key, and the door would unlock. Her thumb found the plastic ridge that outlined the button and traced it, sensing the freedom that came with depressing it.

"Sandy," he said, his impatience growing. His voice shook her out of the daze.

"Yes," she said, and pressed the button.

A metallic click filled the room, and the door slid open an inch. Stale air escaped the gap. All she had to do was open the door the rest of the way, and she could help Greg escape. No turning back now.

She took the handle and pulled reluctantly.

"Finally! Took you long enough." He laughed, and hearing that put her at ease.

She yanked the door open the rest of the way, but something unexpected impeded the door's path.

"What do you think you're doing here?"

She turned and faced the sergeant's squinting eyes.

He sees through my charade.

She thought he saw through the hard woman she pretended to be, saw the young woman who had fallen in love with Greg. Those eyes weighed in on the matter and found her guilty. They accused her of much, forgave her of little.

"Sir—"

"Don't you go making excuses, Masterson." His voice pierced the calm of the laboratory. "I know damn well what you were doing."

She searched his face. Did he know? Was it possible he knew what she had gone through? How much she missed Greg? That she wanted things to go back to how they'd been before all of this?

Eyes twitching, his lips trembled. "You were letting your little buddy go free, weren't you?" His eyes penetrated her. "I asked you a question, soldier. Weren't you?"

"No, Sir." But her answer came out weak and half-hearted. It sounded like a lie because it was a lie. If Greg came out of that cocoon, she would help him. And she would go along with him no matter what came of it.

"Don't you try to deceive me, Masterson."

"Sandy?" Greg asked. "Who's with you?"

The sergeant's eyes zeroed in on the cocoon. "Who the fuck else is here, Masterson?"

Two guards appeared at the entrance to the laboratory. The sergeant waved them off until he said otherwise.

"It's me, Sir," Greg said. "Cooley, Sir."

A look of disbelief fell over the sergeant as his face filled with disgust. "You got to be shitting me."

"No, sir," Sandy said. "It's him." She was hopeful.

His eyes returned to her with stone-cold resolve. "There is no more Cooley, Masterson. There is no form of the Cooley we knew inside of that…*thing*. Look at it, will you? And, you better goddamned get it straight in your head. You got it, Masterson? Do you hear me?"

She didn't have time to respond.

"Sir, it's me," Greg said.

"Shut your pie-hole, beast, or I'll shut it for you."

Sandy looked at the cocoon and felt an urge to run to him. She also knew that there was no way Greg could be inside such a small thing; not the Greg she knew, anyway.

"Get back to your room, Masterson. Now!" He waited for her to retreat then added, "And you can count on this much. I'll have you busted down to a private before break of day for this little foray. I expect you to work hard to regain your rank."

She hung her head in shame and trod back to her room. Both guards followed, snickering quietly between them. There was nothing she could do about it, any of it. She felt helpless.

When they finally called upon her to serve her country, she would. And, she would have nothing to say about it.

Chapter 26

Something poked Sandy's shoulder. It felt soft though, so it wasn't a weapon she had helped to develop. Fingers, maybe, but not from a creature.

Fuzzy headed, she rolled over and saw Nancy looking down at her.

"What?" Sandy asked.

The frustration of lost sleep had come through in her tone. Sandy needed sleep more than ever. In part thanks to Nancy's blow to her head, the very person now waking her. More so because she hadn't slept well in a very long time.

"Look," Nancy said, pointing at something on the horizon.

Sandy rolled to her side. Once strong muscles, her ribs felt somewhat tender now. She wished she could heal faster. The atrophy was significant, thanks to her malnutrition. Her eyes strained to bring anything into clarity, but soon realized she saw nothing out of the ordinary. She stared up at Nancy, wondering if the woman was seeing things.

"There," Nancy said. A frown pressed on the woman's lips; she drew a clear line in the air with her finger. Sandy traced the finger's path to its destination.

"I see nothing," Sandy said.

Nancy leaned over Sandy's body and pointed her finger out from Sandy's perspective. She adjusted the height, the angle, trying to bring what she saw into a direct line for Sandy to see. Then, Sandy did see, and it completely surprised her. There was some activity on the horizon, something bobbing up and down, someone or something approaching them.

"What is that?" Sandy asked, unsure if Nancy knew or not.

"No idea, but it's gotten bigger over the last half-hour."

Sandy peered at the object, observing it for a while in silence, wishing she had a pair of binoculars. She steadied her head on Bernard's pack. Funny how easy it had been for him to leave it behind, as if he no longer required material items. Sandy imagined she hadn't noticed the pack as she believed Nancy would have said something by now. Or maybe she had seen it and was only ignoring the pack for personal reasons. Denial, maybe—the notion he might return for it. He wouldn't, though, because Sandy knew he was no longer the Bernard they knew. He was the other Bernard, the one they had encountered during that last battle, after Sandy killed him, a mere puppet to his master.

If she had the brass to breech those details with Nancy, she would need proof, of which she had little. The only proof she had, Nancy could not see—an ability she could neither prove nor disprove to Nancy. And Sandy fully thought the woman would believe anything to the contrary, so long as it meant Bernard would come back to her. That skepticism would exist even if Bernard showed up, professing his undying love to Nancy while holding a bloody machete behind his back. Sandy was sure Nancy would run right into his murderous arms.

"I think it's people," Sandy whispered, suddenly aware their voices might carry.

Nancy and Bernard had informed her how few people remained after the war with the aliens. Most survivors stuck to more resourceful terrain, like those near waterways. There would be plenty of free real estate scattered along every shoreline. Those who stuck to more central locations would end up like Bernard and Nancy, packed together in small communities by rivers. The people they all needed to stay wary of were the pillagers. In every crisis, there were people not to trust but even they stuck to groups, very few people wanting to be on their own.

"Should we leave?" Nancy asked.

Sandy tried to make out the silhouettes, looking for anything that suggested they might be friendly. "I think we should get packed up, just in case."

"And then what?" Nancy was already packing.

Sandy realized there was more to her packing than fear of these unknown people. Surely it was the notion that they might go looking for Bernard. Sandy knew that wasn't an option, though. They couldn't anywhere near that town as long as Jake was there, and Marty wasn't. If she finally went back, she wouldn't do so ill prepared, as that would have dire consequences.

"I'd say we wait as long as we can," Sandy said, "see if they're friendly or not. If can't determine that soon, though, we leave quickly and stay well ahead of them."

"Does that mean—"

"We'll—" Sandy cut her off before she could even get the question out. She didn't want to feed Nancy's urgency about finding her man. "We'll go around."

For all Sandy knew, Bernard was already dead. Nancy and he had been lucky to have so much time together. If it weren't for Sandy, they wouldn't even have that. But this would always happen.

"Are you sure?" Nancy asked.

Sandy watched the hazy bumps spring up all around them. Some of them might have been alone, but most stuck to large groups. She rubbed her eyes, wishing this was just some illusion.

"Jesus Christ," Sandy said.

"Right? They're everywhere."

Sandy didn't know how to respond. Some of these people were closer than the others. Sandy squinted, trying to bring them into focus.

"I think I see a...dog," Nancy said.

Chapter 27

Ike didn't like this one bit. Bento's howling had woken them, which put them both on immediate guard. When they got to their feet and saw the multitude of people around them, Ike nearly crapped himself, though that dog's barking alone had nearly caused that.

Bento barked as he ran up to one group. Then the dog crossed to another, his muzzle close to the backs of their legs. One man looked down, his eyes glazed over, but he didn't bother to scold the dog. The two women walking with the man ignored Bento altogether.

Ike scratched his ass. "What the literal fuck—"

Marty's hand closed, then opened, appearing anxious for his sword. Ike couldn't blame him and kind of wished he had a sword at this point. But Marty didn't reach for his sword. Instead, he went for a gun.

Well, thank God.

Only Marty's gun looked like none he had seen before. It was old and worn and looked like it would misfire the second Marty used it.

Why would Marty bring a broken gun?

No, it would fire. And Ike had to admit, Marty looked like a bit of a badass holding that old pistol. He gave off a real cowboy-like vibe these days—well, more like a cowboy ninja vibe, but it was still cool. But Ike didn't get the whole ponytail look at all. Thinking of it, many jokes came to mind. They ranged from demented jests to flat-out insults. Sure, Ike had seen plenty of ponytails in his life. Hell, dozens of little girls had them back in the days before the attack. But he had yet to see a single one on any man he considered being a straight man, especially at Marty's age. Above all, he just liked teasing Marty, and he thought Marty kind of got a kick out of it, too. Now was no exception.

"Maybe you could ponytail them all to death." Ike chuckled. "They'd all die of freaking laughter."

Marty shot him a look, then he laughed, lowering the gun. After a few chuckles, Marty placed the gun in the holster at his hip.

"What? Why are you putting that thing away?"

"They couldn't care less about us."

Ike watched the people, taking time to reflect on each one. All of them wore the same blank expression. They stared off into the distance, looking as though they were sleepwalking, yet they were all awake.

Bento stopped barking when Marty whistled for him. The dog trotted between the groups of people, appearing nervous. His tongue slid in and out as he panted, making the dog seem rather crazy from these people's sudden appearance. The dog whined, displaying his displeasure.

Marty only studied the dog. "They're all part of this," Marty said. "Tied in to him."

"What the hell do you mean?"

Marty sighed. Ike knew what was bothering him even before he answered. "Like Sheila."

"Oh shit, Marty, you think—"

"Yes."

"Holy fuckarama." Ike followed the footsteps of a man who was much bigger and stronger than even Bernard. "You mean it's us versus them?"

Marty tugged at his beard. "I'm not sure, but maybe."

"Why on Earth would he need all these people?"

"Well," Marty said, still tugging at those hairs on his chin. "I suppose they're all just chess pieces to him." His fingers pinched the hairs, tugging them harder. "But I'd guess this is in large for me. He's building the stronger country."

Ike ignored this last part, unable to grasp its relevance.

"Shit, he doesn't need this many people to get one old pony-tailed bastard like you, does he?"

Marty stared at him. Could Marty hold his own against so many people? And if he could, then why the hell did he need Ike? The answer came to Ike suddenly.

Because the stakes are too great.

Marty could never do this alone as long as she was in danger. Realizing this, Ike wondered what Marty expected of him. He considered what Marty might ask of him. That concerned Ike more than anything. Somehow, he had exposed Marty's greatest weakness. Surely Jake would know it, too.

Chapter 28

The emotion Bernard experienced upon hearing his voice was intense. The word Jake spoke brought it on like a wave in the ocean, crashing against him, an undeniable force. When the word pierced his thoughts, Bernard could think of only one thing. He had to get to Jake—only he wasn't Jake any longer. He had to get to the Infinite.

His thoughts turned to Nancy; how hurt she had looked. He had felt those eyes tracking his progress for a long while but had ignored her despite how much he still loved her. That alone was the reason he had let her live. He had wanted to make sure Sandy was dead, but there hadn't been time, especially with Nancy pawing at him to stay. He hoped the woman was dead. She was a threat. Now that he heard the Infinite, none of that mattered. He could think of nothing but the network, of who was calling for him, of finally reaching and standing before the Infinite.

Nancy's words were meaningless, only an irritating pest. The Infinite would deal with Sandy later if he deemed it necessary. For the moment, the only command had been, "Now," and Bernard intended to get there as soon as possible.

Somewhere high above him, perhaps thousands of miles away, there were other plans being attended to. There would be no more of those ugly aliens. The Infinite would ensure that, as he was in full control of both the heavens and the Earth. Bernard would do his part.

He hadn't noticed those joining him on this journey. He wondered what they would do, what things the Infinite had in store for them. If nothing else, maybe he would place Bernard back into a cell. That delighted Bernard, as the cell was like a strong drug. Like any other addiction, once cured, the bliss it brought never really went away. It haunted, begging for another taste.

In those cells, nothing could harm him. He lived only the best life, a never-ending tale. In the cell, Bernard could be a king. He could be a hero, and he belonged there. But only if the Infinite saw it fit for him.

Bernard walked with purpose. He shed the life of a mortal like a snake's dead skin. With the help of the Infinite, he would begin this next life. He placed his trust in the hands of his master.

Chapter 29

Sometimes the Infinite's life felt perfect. He remembered the first time he tended to the fields on his own, long before Marty came to live with him. It had felt good to be in charge, a master of all he surveyed. Once Marty burst onto the scene, his presence had somehow soured that satisfaction. The accomplishment no longer belonged to *only* him because it was their farm then.

But what frustrated Jake most was the bad hip. The way the doctors hadn't been able to make it work right. How the injury had kept him from those fields for so long. Once that happened, everything he had worked toward, all the pride, all went to Marty. He kind of despised Marty for that, and how his brother had always babied him.

No, it wasn't Marty's fault.

Nothing was ever Marty's fault. Their parents had engrained that fact into his head long ago. Yet, Marty had worked on the farm. Marty was always the one who kept going, gaining strength and a winning spirit. His brother always succeeded where he failed.

Now as the Infinite, he had the power to change all that. This was more than a need. It came out of greed. This was selfish. And the Infinite was okay with that. Even the part of him that was still Jake agreed with that notion.

Now, sitting in front of Marty's woman, the Infinite felt more powerful than ever. "Tell me, Sheila," he said, "What is our Marty like these days?"

She stared at him, an empty expression pasted on her face. "I... I don't—"

"I mean, what has he been up to, Sheila?" The Infinite grinned. She had such a weak mind.

"He means to kill you. It's all he's trained for since last time."

This shouldn't surprise the Infinite, yet it did. His brother had already expressed his distaste for a merging. Marty even tried to kill him—twice even. After all those wrongdoings, hearing her relay this detail to him still stung.

"Kill me?" he asked.

"Yes, my Infinite."

He enjoyed hearing his name on her lips. Perhaps if Marty bothered him with this killing matter too much, he would just take his brother's woman for his own. He would dangle her out there to rub it in. No way Marty could deny his power then.

The Jake part of him protested the thought.

The Infinite ignored his human side, dwelling on the concept. The Infinite did not require love. Nor did he desire sex. A woman's touch meant little to him. Sheila's body and sultry voice did not differ from any other meat bag to him. She was nothing but flesh, but power was a whole other matter.

The Infinite desired power over these meat bags. He could control them, use some of them for energy and use others to appease the human side that continued to infest his thoughts. This would suffice until he severed that other half. Once the Infinite discovered a means to achieve that, he would no longer require any companionship. Until then, they would have to remain as his pets.

Power, indeed.

He studied Sheila's face. She had strength, too. Securing her as one of his many possessions gave him unequivocal superiority over Marty. His brother would crumble before him if he knew what things the Infinite could do to her. Yet, she still had her secret, one the Infinite hadn't uncovered.

Sheila's hands moved to her stomach, out of instinct it seemed. There, they rested upon the slight swell of her tummy. The Infinite observed this with interest, thinking she might be hungry. Hunger was an unfortunate side effect of being human, and he could provide food if she required it.

No, it's not hunger.

The palms of her hands flattened against the sides of her belly. She rubbed her stomach in slow circles. A small, telling smile formed on her lips.

A smile? What a vile act.

Then the Infinite understood everything.

"Tell me of yourself, Sheila. Do you have any secrets?"

Her face flushed a bright red; a telltale sign that she was guilty as charged. "Secret?"

"Yes, dear. Maybe something you've kept from Marty?"

"Yes, I have a secret." He could sense her struggle to maintain composure as he pried this information out of her. "My...my baby." She no doubt feared for her child's life.

"Oh my, my. Brother has been a busy little bee, hasn't he?"

Sheila didn't answer.

No matter. Now he had more power over Marty than he originally thought. His brother would stand at his side, like it or not. Marty would never let his wife suffer, but a baby would only cement that fate.

Chapter 30

Bento—as the man referred to him—looked up at the man he now called Master. He was such a good man. Bento had known that from the first time they met.

Scanning their surroundings, there were dozens of other men and women. None of them were good.

He spotted a rabbit.

The urge to give chase overwhelmed Bento. He wanted to kill the rabbit. Why, he did not know, but the desire was strong. Somehow, he ignored the desire.

He looked back at Master. Good. He was still there. Still safe. He hoped Master would end the pain all these people caused Bento. At first, it had only been a slight pain. Back then it had made him howl more than anything—hearing that word over and over. Now he heard so many words, and all at once. Hearing all that scared Bento, and all these people made him nervous. But the pain that resulted from it all was becoming unbearable.

Bento—or Max, as his previous owner once called him—missed home. Not the home where Master found him, but his old home, the one with his old Master. Things had been easier. There had been bones and squeaky toys and meaty treats and food. At least he had this new Master, and although he missed his old family, he loved his new Master, too. He was a good man

All these voices confused Bento. These men and women didn't move their mouths, but he heard them speaking all the same. Their thoughts were loud, and they were all frightened, like Bento was of thunder. More than anything, he wanted to bite their ankles, one by one. Maybe that would keep their voices out of his head. Master might disapprove. Maybe seeing that would even scare Master. He didn't want to disappoint Master.

Sometimes, Bento wondered if he would ever go through that feeling again, where his whole body shook and trembled uncontrollably. He worried what had happened, that it might happen again. It haunted his dreams.

He looked at Master's friend. He didn't like the smell of the man, but that was different. He couldn't hear the man's voice like he had Master's woman. Bento tolerated the man and his ugly face.

Master had a kind face. He did kind things, like rub Bento's cheeks or his belly. But Bento could sense the fear in Master.

Bento wished he could calm Master down. To make him happy. He wouldn't mind if they went back to Master's woman even and wished he could express this to Master. But how?

He barked.

Master smiled at him.

The attention made Bento feel good. Perhaps, Master had heard him. Maybe he understood his words. Then Master looked away, and Bento wasn't so sure. Worried, Bento thought about the one thing he felt more than anything right now.

Love Master.

Once wasn't enough, though. Bento flooded his thoughts with the words.

Love Master. Love Master. Love Master.

Suddenly, Master was looking at him again. Only he wasn't smiling. His expression looked strange. Bento didn't like that. All he wanted was to make Master happy.

Bento barked.

Master shook his head and smiled at Bento.

This thrilled Bento.

Chapter 31

They gathered around the Infinite, both those who were of him and those who were not. Of the latter, some thought him a god. The majority remained in doubt. Who could blame them after what they had been through? He would convince them all. Even if he found himself unable to achieve this end, he would just take them. But he had already raised the dead. That should have been enough. That had been convincing enough that many already thought him the prophetic return of their lord. But it hadn't won them all over. So, he needed something more convincing.

That first miracle came thanks to the advanced alien technology he had surgically implanted inside of him during a long and complex procedure. What he was about to attempt should convince the rest, or at least enough of them to make his job easier. This was something only he could do, a result of this metamorphic change on top of the implant—a good trick.

They stood around him like sheep at pasture, all of them appearing unsure of what would happen, ignorant to the many possibilities. The Infinite liked their comparison of him to their Jesus and wondered if their Jesus might have felt similar whenever he had addressed the masses. Did messiahs like that feel power?

Part of him would always find something morally wrong with what the Infinite was doing. Yet it thrilled him how effortless it was to fool these people. Deep inside, the protests had grown silent these last few hours, but he knew Jake detested all he did. But, perhaps, good old Jake was weakening.

Or was Jake just resting up, the need to conserve energy taking precedence over protest? He couldn't decide, but, whatever the case, Jake's silence was most welcomed. Perhaps the end of Jake was not far behind.

"Show us the way, oh Lord," one woman said.

The Infinite ignored her, encouraging the crowd to come closer.

"He's not a god," one man said. Still, that man followed the others, curious or otherwise.

"Shush, Harold," another woman said. She followed close behind the very man she had just scolded.

More than twenty people gathered around the Infinite for his newest miracle. But more were coming. Many more. All those people were still under his control from last time, those he had reached out to once the network cleared. These fresh meat bags would soon join those forces.

Already he could see their heads bobbing up and down on the horizon. Seeing them, the Infinite set this part of his plan into motion.

"Am I not?" The Infinite struck a finger at the man and shook it in defiance. The man looked uncomfortable under the Infinite's judging gaze. "What know ye of gods and men?"

The man, a bundle of nerves, didn't answer.

Calm fell over the crowd. Sheila and a few others already into the Infinite's network, loomed along the outer edge of the gathering. They would do whatever he asked of them. Knowing that made him feel cozy, realizing that no matter how things turned out, he would maintain control.

Several men and women still lingered in town. Some tended to their daily chores, trying to make up for the work lost by those who surrounded the Infinite. They paid little attention now, but soon enough, there would be no choice. Once the Infinite had these people under his control, he would just take the others if need be. No one could stop him from stripping every resource from this planet for good.

"I...I'm sorry, Lord," the woman who had hushed Harold said.

The Infinite nodded, a smile forming on his face. It was

genuine, as he wanted to laugh. He held it back. There would be time for laughter later, when he was alone. For now, all he needed to concern himself with was the show.

"In fact," the Infinite said, extending his palms outward as if embracing the entire town. He spoke loud enough for all to hear. "What do any of you know more than I?" His eyes found each of them, seeing a few more people break away from their work. They would be next. "Ye build, when you should follow me to the gates of Heaven!"

"Amen, Lord. Amen!" This man fell to his knees before the Infinite.

"Have thee seen God? Or God's son? Are you so sure I am not he?"

The Infinite shook his hands. He still couldn't understand how they could doubt him after that last miracle. Had he underestimated how easy it would be to convince all the meat bags of this notion? Either way, he would have, regardless of their lack of beliefs.

"No, Lord," a woman said.

It was Tia. He focused on her, playing upon her weak will. "Has thee seen me? Has thee not seen the face of God's son come back to lead the way for thee?"

The woman crumbled to her knees. Fresh tears sprinkled her cheeks, which flushed a rosy red. She let her hands fall to the ground before her and bowed to the Infinite.

Oh yes, he liked this very much.

"Yes, Lord." She traced an invisible cross on her chest and bowed again.

"Then why do thy brothers and sisters not see me for who I truly am? Shall they not be my children?" Again, he cast guilt upon those unwilling to join him. The act reeled in two more, who approached with some obvious reservation.

Tia rose to her knees and gazed at those who were not present. The Infinite could see her anger coming to a boil. A similar angst brewed in the others. Without doubt, if he couldn't have them now, he would have them later.

"Ted, get your aaaa—" The man shot a sorrowful glance to the Infinite for the improper word. "Join us, Ted. Come."

Some young man the Infinite presumed to be Ted looked up from his work long enough to acknowledge the man calling for him. All he did was shake his head before consuming himself back in his work.

"Will no more of my children come to my side in the end of days?" the Infinite asked out loud. He held his hands to the sky, shook them with fierce intent, and a low rumble of thunder came in response.

Truthfully, he hadn't planned on that. Had no way of achieving that even, but he was thankful for the touch of profound drama Mother Nature added to his show. It got the attention of a few other doubters.

He put the final touches on. "Forgive them, God," and he lowered his eyes, "for they know not what they do."

A chorus of whispers spread through the crowd. Those surrounding him looked unsettled by the ignorance of the others. Now, he would give them a miracle, a little trick he had discovered on his own while trying to forget the static that once disrupted his network. He raised both hands, preparing them for something spectacular. His fingers spread and trembled as he tried to make it look as though he was drawing something out of the soil. Men and women clamored around him, their whispers growing louder.

This all drew new interest from those who hadn't yet joined them. One more man came, and that made the Infinite smile. Every meat bag that joined his cause made this a little easier. His wraps blew in the wind, as he began to conjure a food of sorts. It was of his creation, and thus of his nature. This was his body, his soul. Those who ate of his bread would be of his will.

A grumble rose from deep inside of him, not caring for the comparison being made. The Infinite ignored Jake. This was the Infinite's Kool-Aid, the drink he would serve his masses.

"Join me, my children," he said, letting his voice carry over them and to everyone else. He raised his hands, and when he did, little bluish mushroom-like caps began to sprout from the ground. "Join me and eat of the food I provide thee." Only they weren't mushrooms. He made them look pleasant to eat. "Join me in eating my bread."

Everyone kept their distance at first, somewhat hesitant to accept the miracle. They whispered among themselves, some of it even in blasphemy. This didn't concern the Infinite yet, though. He remained poised, expressing a giving nature.

Finally, one by one, a few entered his circle of creation. They each bent and secured a cap. Others knelt and ate quickly. Hums of satisfaction filled the air. As their approval of the food found the others, they joined them. Nearly the entirety of these people ate of his creation. The Infinite remained patient even when those who refused to eat, turned away.

Sheila blocked one man's path, preventing him from leaving. A few others who had already eaten and connected to the Infinite's network did their best to contain the others. As they ate, dozens of fresh meat bags joined the network. All of this pleased the Infinite. And they continued to eat until he gave the command.

Now.

All these new people stood and moved as one. They moved upon those who hadn't eaten, circling them, forcing them to the center of the crowd. All protests went ignored.

"I'm not eating this shit," one woman said.

The Infinite smiled as two of his men took her arms. She tried to free herself of their grasp but failed. One of the Infinite's female meat bags grabbed a blue cap and force-fed it to the woman. The woman spat it out, as if it were poison. They fed the woman another, and this time, the Infinite's female meat bag held the woman's mouth shut. The woman coughed and snorted, doing whatever she could to keep from inhaling the cap. The same fate fell upon all who hadn't eaten. Some ate under this pressure, some still resisted. They held their breath or tried to force it out, but once it became lodged in their throat, it was choke to death or swallow. They all gave in. When they did, they felt the release. One man turned a deep shade of blue before he gave in but give in he did. Once all had eaten, the Infinite gave the command again.

Now.

This small victory satisfied him. In a single day, he had taken most of this community and turned them. They would follow him anywhere. Treat him like a god. Above all, they would do as he wished. His will be done.

Chapter 32

The next wave of people showing up made the Infinite ecstatic. More would come, of course, but for now, there were enough of them to take over the small village with ease. Before this came to fruition, though, he decided he needed a little rest, if for no other reason than to reflect upon his impending victory. Ruling could be a tiring task.

He retired to his shack and sat at the table, looking over the meal they had prepared for him. Dragging the fork through the slop displeased him, the colors and textures appearing so bland. He imagined how it must taste, trying to access Jake's memories. Potatoes were an awful creation, leaving a grainy sensation in the mouth he had trouble getting rid of. Carrots were much too sweet for his well-defined palate. This plate had a good-sized chunk of meat, too. He hated meat, and it made him happy to know he would never have to eat it again.

The Infinite was thankful no one bothered him this time. Now that he had some control over them, he could keep them away. He sat alone, which was good, and lifted one hand above the table, pretending to shake the fingers as if straining. On the table, he produced one blue cap. The sound of suction accompanied the act of plucking it from the surface, as if it had somehow rooted itself to the wood grain. He held the cap in his hands and studied it.

It began to change, shifting in his hand as he struggled to maintain a firm hold of it. The color remained blue with crimson red veins spread throughout be its translucent body. Light pulses of energy surged through the tiny creature. The

Infinite liked the way it looked, as it was a small part of his own being. The creature struggled against his fingers, pulling and pushing, attempting to escape. Unable to free itself of his grasp, it did the one thing instinctual to any organism when trapped—it bit.

The Infinite laughed, observing the creature's struggle as it tore away a strip of flesh between his thumb and forefinger. The wound quickly healed over. And every time the small organism opened up a new wound, it, too, healed over with ease. This did nothing to discourage the creature who became insatiable in its need for safety. The Infinite saw the begrudging creature back on the table, and, for a moment, it calmed. When it finally tried to escape, the Infinite brought his hand down fast, crushing it with his flattened palm. Purple globs of jelly-like blood sprayed across the table. The Infinite laughed hysterically.

Small things like this pleased him most. His ability to control life or death amused him. Having learned much existence, this knowledge of himself made him consider his own existence.

Maybe I really am a god.

Surely, he wasn't the god these people knew, the one many of them had read about in books. And he was not a forgiving creator. His rule would be one of hardship, challenging his people to serve their master, the all-powerful Infinite. He would be a giver of life as much as he would be a bringer of death.

He lifted his hand. Strands of the sticky goo dripped from the digits. The Infinite concentrated, and, with a little extra effort, his hand glowed the beautiful orange color again. The color matched his eyes well. As the illumination intensified, he thought about the first time he had discovered this ability, back on his ship. This was the ability that had given him power over his alien adversaries. Thinking of them now, he scanned the network, unafraid of what he shared. There he found the news he sought. The alien race would never trouble him again. He would rebuild their empire as his own and expand upon it. The Infinite would create life in his image. That was what gods did.

A burst of light from beneath his hand. When the flash dissipated, the strange creature he had killed moments earlier stood unsettled, brought back from the dead. The Infinite studied the confused, simple-minded organism. If he let it grow, he knew it would become an intelligent creature. But he didn't have the luxury to wait for that to happen just yet.

With the organism still stunned by its sudden resurrection, he picked it up. Once it understood its fate, the creature struggled against the Infinite's grasp. Only this time escape was futile.

He held the creature close to his eyes, the Infinite looked around, making sure no one was around. Convinced he was alone, he let his image fade. His body which appeared as a simple, clean-looking man, turned an icy translucent color. His flesh looked like a cool evening pool of water. Inside his body, a network of veins pulsed with electric surges up and down, almost like tiny spaceships in a vast universe. He felt his face change, but remained patient, waiting for the transformation to finish before he ate. When it did, he tossed the small organism into his mouth and swallowed it whole without hesitation, satisfying his appetite.

Chapter 33

Ted Strom leaned against the back of the makeshift house where the miracle worker lived and recalled everything he had been through, the aliens, all of it. Had he chosen the wrong path? The end of days would come—he knew that—so he needed to be sure about his decision. It was hard to deny what he had seen, the things this self-proclaimed Lord had already done. Might he do more?

Ted had never been much of a spiritual man. In fact, he had only just gotten beyond some of his wildest years when the aliens ruined everything. He had been out of college for years but still lived that party life to the fullest. Ted took the catastrophe as a sign he should settle down, and fast.

Many had done a better job at re-establishing themselves than Ted. Some people had makeshift power, which he had heard over his radio. Of this he couldn't be certain, as the words came jumbled right before the batteries gave in for good. But he liked to believe the old world was slowly coming back. That gave him hope.

He supposed he could always make his way into town, pick up some replacement batteries and try to tune in the signal all over again. Sometimes he wished it had an AC adapter, so he could just plug in his radio and wait for the power to come back on. But what did it matter, anyway? It could have been anyone, someone fooling around or dabbling in matters they shouldn't be, an accidental discovery. Besides, it wasn't like he would go seek them out. He suspected all the *real* power was being reserved.

Occasionally, they would all glimpse this power. Perhaps the government had made it through everything, taken refuge somewhere deep underground. Having seen many movies on this subject, Ted thought it the precise case. He imagined an entire underground city, capable of housing tens of thousands of government employees, somewhere in the depths below, maybe even at the core of some old inactive volcano. Whatever the case, the regular folks were left to their own devices and barely scraped by.

If this man represented the end of the world, he had to choose carefully. The man was a near perfect specimen, save for the rather large scar around his neck. He wore a tunic fashioned out of a tablecloth and preached words of which Ted knew far too few. Not only this, but the stranger had given life to a dead man. And he had created food where there had been none.

Ted recognized both stories from the Bible. Hadn't Jesus performed these exact acts to prove he had been the Son of God? If true, it would be hard to deny what the man claimed. But no living man or woman knew the truth about those miracles, what they had looked like, to make a fair comparison. So they had to rely on their gut reactions. They had to employ trust. And maybe that was what left Ted in doubt.

He ran his fingers through his hair, trying to comb the stress away. Why was he stressed? He had seen how those who chose to follow the man acted after eating those blue mushrooms. They had even used force on the others, making them eat. And that wasn't just some babble being passed around; he had seen it with his own two eyes.

After they ate, all of them seemed so happy, like they had just gotten back their old lives and were finally happy. That made following the stranger an attractive prospect. Did the special food contain God's word? Had it filled these people with the Holy Spirit? Protected them from harm? If so, that also made him want to eat those odd caps. And Ted wanted to eat. He was hungry, equally so for the promise of what the right decision might bring. It was difficult not to think of it on both planes, too, as while eating would fill his stomach, would it also fill his heart?

Still, he hid, here at the back of the house where he often hid when he didn't want anyone to see him. It was this place that had allowed him to get out of much work. And it afforded him time and space to think, in this case, contemplating whether to go through with this leap of faith.

He had avoided everyone on the way here, feeling like a Judas, defying the will of this savior. He knew many of the stories and suddenly felt an urge to cry. He choked it back—men shouldn't cry. Right when things felt most complicated, something distracted him, and he welcomed it.

An orange glow stole its way out between the boards of the shack. Ted leaned in to the source. Pressing his eye flat against the wood, he shifted from side to side, trying to bring it in to view. There, he saw the stranger, the man who claimed to be their savior, sitting alone at a table. The man held a hand over the table. A colorful goo covered the table beneath the man's hand. His hand trembled as it had when he brought Dave back to life. The intensity grew until a flash came from his palm, so brilliant Ted had to turn his head and rub his eyes clear.

When Ted returned his eye to the crack, he couldn't see the object on the table at first. He believed it a cup, though translucent, like a bottle of water, only darker. Where had this man found such a thing? Then, the object moved.

The man's hand swung down and snatched the thing up. The haze in Ted's eyes subsided, and he saw the small creature struggling in the man's firm grasp. The stranger appeared somewhat amused by this fight, then looked around, before transforming into something else altogether, right before Ted's eyes.

Ted trembled. He struggled to stay afoot, his legs seeming to give all at once. He had to lean against the wall. He had never heard knees knock together—even believed it a silly myth—until now. His heart pounded in his chest as the man's skin became water-like, a deep silvery blue. Small flashes of light shot through his body from finger to shoulder, chest to neck, around the circumference of its head. The now fully transformed stranger stared at the small translucent creature in his hands, and the tiny creature might have growled right then.

The man spread his alien maw, his jaws stretching out to the thing in his hand and attacked the creature like a Venus flytrap might a fly, a sick slurping sound audible even from here.

Turning his head, Ted struggled to hold in the bile gathering in his throat. He didn't want to draw any attention to himself but forced himself to look again. This time the man was as before, the savior so many of them followed so willingly.

Ted yanked his eye away from the wall, still shaken. More and more, all he wanted was to release the sickness in his belly. What he saw terrified him, and he wanted to tell someone, anyone. Would they believe him, though? He considered gathering up some supplies and heading out on his own before he got caught. But he also couldn't help but worry what might transpire in the time it took to gather what he needed. He wondered if he could make it to another town on foot, find some supplies there and get some rest before getting even farther away. That was a more attractive notion.

Looking toward the nearest town, he saw dozens of small bumps on the horizon and wondered what they could be. Whatever they were, he didn't have much time at all.

Ted stumbled away from the wall, almost falling when he did. Concern filled him, and, when he got twenty yards away from the makeshift home, Ted turned and ran.

Chapter 34

Marty was glad to have Ike along. He wished Bernard was here. But, if no one else could be there, Ike would keep Marty from doing the one thing he feared most. Or, at least he hoped Ike would stop him.

Marty's thoughts drifted to the man who had taught him the way of the sword. It was difficult to bring clarity to the memory with all this commotion surrounding them, Bento acting all half-nuts and barking like he was, but Marty forced the image to his thoughts, anyway. Yu had told him, the time for action always came sooner than preferred.

His friendship with the man named Yu Swyi came of a coincidental meeting. Marty thanked his stars for that chance meeting ever since. The man's short, simple name coincided with his beliefs, and his words. Yu had been reluctant at first, back when Marty asked to learn the way of the sword. However, upon hearing Marty's tale, Yu changed his mind, as much of a mystery to Marty as Yu's sudden appearance in this part of the States.

Yu always kept his hair long, thick and black, braided in a tight ponytail. He flipped his hair back over his shoulder when he held the sword out for Marty to see for the first time.

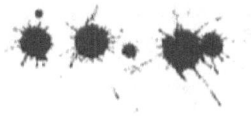

"This is a special sword." Yu held it in both hands, offering it to Marty.

Marty didn't think now the right time to take the sword. He would need to earn this privilege.

A wrinkle furled on Yu's forehead. "What are you doing?"

"Looking at the sword."

"Well, why aren't you picking it up?" Even with the accent, Yu's English was good.

Marty's cheeks flushed, and he took the sword. He supposed the time for formalities had passed with the hives. Yu wanted him to get a good look at the sword, and Marty couldn't help but chuckle as he observed it, having derived the notion from watching too many late-night movies. The sword was lighter than he expected, and shorter. He took the black leather-bound handle in his palm and wrapped his fingers around it. The sword felt comfortable in his hand, as if it belonged there. He studied the delicate red ribbon wrapped around the scabbard. Light purple letters lined the ribbon, spelling out a message in a language Marty couldn't read.

Yu wore an amused grin. He demonstrated how to withdraw the sword from its scabbard. Marty watched, then repeated the action, not all the way but far enough to see the etching on one side of the blade.

"What does this mean?" Marty asked.

Yu looked at the etching, though Marty suspected he didn't need to. It was probable he had memorized the words, yet, still Yu's eyes thinned on the markings, as if trying to read them. His dark hair wavered in a light breeze as he gazed out across the decimated cityscape. "Not yet, my friend." He sounded distant, as if lost in his memories. He turned back to Marty. "That is a lesson for another day. First, we learn patience and precision. We honor our sword."

Yu took the sword back, knelt, and laid out a red cloth. He

began to disassemble the sword. Marty watched as Yu carefully took the special sword apart, laying the pieces out on the cloth. When he finished, he beckoned Marty closer, and began to describe each piece. Marty listened, intent on remembering his words, the pattern in which he placed them.

As Yu picked up the first piece, he pulled a yellow silk rag from his pocket. He turned the piece in his hands, wiping it clean as he described it to Marty. When Yu finished cleaning it, he placed the piece back on the cloth. He did the same with every piece until everything was cleaned. Then, Yu reassembled the sword, and returned it to its scabbard.

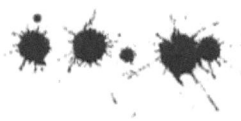

An abrupt bark shook Marty from the memory. He glanced down at Bento and smiled. This was a special dog. Marty was lucky to have found him.

Bento seemed distracted by all these people. All of them looked as though hypnotized. He wanted to rid the Earth of them now but knew heading down that would eventually see him killing someone he loved, and several other acquaintances. He had already failed at taking this road once before, so he didn't think it would not serve him well to try it again.

Love Master.

Marty looked around. Who said that?

His gaze fell on Bento. Had Bento spoken to him? Marty stared long and hard at the dog, weighing whether this was possible. Was it? Given the strange circumstances of the dog, maybe.

The dog barked.

Marty's weak grin grew. Bento had said nothing. It must have been from some memory, something residual in his thoughts, Master Yu's teaching or the like.

He allowed himself to drift back to the memory of the man.

Before he could submerse himself back in the past, he saw them. On the horizon, two women waited, and Marty recognized Nancy right away. The other woman eluded him, but it was so good to see Nancy again. But where was Bernard?

Chapter 35

Sandy ran for Marty, tripped over a large rock protruding from the ground, and face planted to the ground hard enough to create a raspberry on her left cheek. All she could do was laugh, given her clumsiness. It was a good sign how much muscle she had lost during her time on the ship. But it was also good to see Marty.

Marty hurried to her, Ike directly behind him.

"Who do we have here, Marty old pal?" Ike asked.

"Shut it, Ike," Sandy said in playful warning.

"Oh, I see," Ike said, a coy grin spreading across his lips. "It's that young bitch, Masterson, again, eh?"

Sandy laughed. Weirdly, she always liked Ike. Sure, sometimes he was a real pain in the ass, but he had a way of making a tough pill a little easier to swallow.

Marty took her by the elbow and helped her to her feet. He examined the brush-burn closely. "It's not too bad."

"I'm fine." Sandy knocked Marty's probing hands away.

He recoiled, a moment of self-doubt, perhaps. She assuaged any worry he might have with a long hug, squeezing so hard she could hear the air escape Marty in a wheeze.

"It's *so* good to see you again," Sandy said into the unwashed threads of Marty's shirt. Her fingers discovered some odd thing strapped to his back, what she thought was one of the shock-sticks. Her hands traced its contour and once she realized what it really was, she couldn't help but feel a little disappointed.

Something else poked at her hip. A gun.

That's more like it.

Marty pushed her away. "It's good to see you, too, kiddo. Where have you been?"

Sandy's eyes drifted upward.

"Jesus fucking Christ," Ike said.

She agreed with that sentiment.

"Are you okay?" Marty observed the wound on her head. "I mean...are you okay?" his hands remained frozen, as if wanting to help with her wounds but unsure if he should.

"That was my doing." Nancy said and took a sheepish step toward Marty, extending a hand.

"Nancy. It's good to see you." Marty shooed the hand away and gave her a big hug. "Well, whatever happened, it seems you two sorted out your differences, correct?"

They both nodded.

"Good," Marty said. "Now, where's Bernard?"

Nancy started tearing up, and Marty's face flushed. Not because Bernard wasn't there but because of what he associated with the man's absence.

"Sheila?" Sandy asked, already knowing the answer.

Marty shrugged, trying to act like it didn't bother him.

Ike stepped forward and gave Sandy a one-handed hug, and it was awkward. But that brought back her smile. He gave Nancy a similar hug. Something about the man felt different. He was still crusty all around the edges but perhaps his filling—so to say—had softened a bit.

"And who is this?" Sandy asked.

The dog wagged its tail, peeking out between Marty's legs, whimpering as it gawked at Sandy with wide eyes. There was no need for Marty to tell her his name, though. Somehow, she got it right away.

"This is fucking Bento," Ike said. "Likes to lick his nuts and all. Damn if I don't admire him for that ability. Hell, I'd never leave home if I could like my nuts."

Sandy shot him a look of disgust, one matched by Nancy. All Ike did was laugh. He likely missed their little back and forth as much as she did.

She snapped her fingers at the dog, begging him to come closer. Bento hid behind Marty's leg.

Seeing this, Marty sighed. "He's—"

"I know," Sandy said. "He can see the other me."

She looked up at Marty, saw the way he his eyes searched her. He looked different, younger maybe. A man with a purpose.

"Did you see all those people?" he asked.

"Yes," Nancy said. "Let's not talk about all that."

Sandy knew why. Nancy didn't want to discuss the truth about what happened to Bernard. It would sour the moment.

"I'm afraid we will have to, Nancy."

Marty scanned the field, and Sandy did the same. Only a few bumps unsettled on the grassy horizon. She hoped that was the last of them, at least for now. Surely, more would come.

How many?

A gathering had begun.

Chapter 36

Ike thought Sandy looked rather underfed. Even with her being all skin and bones, she still looked like she could kick his ass. But something about her seemed different. Maybe her eyes didn't have that quickness they once had, or she didn't look as strong or whatever. No, now he saw it. She was a smart woman, maybe even now, but some of those wires in her head had gotten crossed and shorted out the whole circuit breaker.

Nancy didn't look so great, either. He well knew what problems plagued her, and already he could see the only thing she really cared about was getting her Bernard back. That was the very reason they hadn't trusted her last time, her obsession with Bernard even when they all knew he was being controlled by Marty's brother. And that was the reason they couldn't trust her now.

Still, she had come through last time, hadn't she? But that crazed look in her eyes troubled him in a way different from Sandy's loose wires. Nancy had the potential to be dangerous.

Ike wasn't sure there was anything potentially more hazardous than meeting up with two crazy broads. Here they would storm the castle, and all they had to fight by their side was these two flaky nut-jobs. At any moment, one might try to take the other's head, or anyone else's. And what if Sandy sold them out to the aliens? She had been gone for long enough, up there on their ship. Might she have been compromised? And what about Nancy? She would sell them out in a heartbeat if it meant she could be with Bernard again. Truth told, he didn't trust either of them. Life sure could be a bitch when a woman lost her wits. Lucky for Ike, he now had two such women traveling with him.

Realizing they had been talking with him zoned out the entire time, Ike said, "So, what did you eat?"

"Ike?" Nancy said. "Didn't you hear her answer that very question several minutes ago?"

He didn't care for being scolded by nut-bag number one. "Nah, guess I missed that. Guess I was too fucking busy worrying about the fact we're up to our knees in some bad shit...again." He faked smile at Nancy.

Bento came up beside him. Ike leaned away when the dog tried to lick his hand. No way he wanted that dog's freaking ball sack germs all over him. Besides, dogs made him nervous. What if it started barking in the middle of the night and gave away their position to someone terrible? Sure, those bastards already knew their general location, given the sheer number of idiots that passed by earlier, but that didn't mean it wasn't best to keep on the down-low, just in case. That damn dog was yapping like crazy when it saw all those people. What if it got crazy like that right before they attacked Jake?

Dogs and bitches, man. Both are unpredictable as hell. Ike reconsidered this thought. *Except for Becca.*

There was also Marty to worry about. He was sure he could rely on Marty so long as Sheila didn't get in the way. Even then, Ike was positive Sheila would somehow end up being a distraction.

What Ike worried about was so simple he could play the scene out in his thoughts. He could see them attacking, old ass Marty leading the way, wielding a sword and some old pistol, his ponytail flopping in the breeze. The overly pale-assed Sandy would follow right behind, wanting to lead them but too weak to be any threat. Nancy would see Bernard and wouldn't hesitate to scurry her butt right over to him. Then, a split second before their dysfunctional force struck, that damn dog would bark and ruin everything. No doubt Ike's old, wrinkly ass would bring up the rear, offering him a great view of their failure.

A real fuckarama.

Ike tuned back into the conversation in time to hear Sandy

discussing the aliens and quickly tuned back out. She really seemed to love talking about those fucking aliens. Gift of gab or otherwise, Ike thought maybe all that time alone would make anyone want to talk your ears off. But Ike made no mistake about it; this woman remained focused on the mission. She didn't care what it took to get to the end, but she fully intended to finish this business.

"So, for my turn," Sandy said, "several months after the others, they gave me a highly experimental serum."

"What do you mean...experimental?" Marty asked.

She nodded, signifying it was a fair question. "Well, by then our little test had already accidently taken hold on your brother. But, they were sure they had narrowed down which strain of the original serum caused the transformations. They removed those strands and injected me with the end product. There was some real concern the concoction might be toxic, but nothing like that ever kept them from testing on people before, especially for little old me, the one who had already let them down. And I suppose I didn't much care anymore, either."

"Fuck! That's some real shit right there," Ike said, not sure he wanted to rejoin the conversation.

"You bet it is." Nancy's eyes darted over her shoulder.

She wasn't keeping an eye out for bad guys. What she wanted to see was Bernard. Like the big lug would have a sudden change of heart.

Not a frigging chance.

"Well, I had to go through all this extra training in case it did work. In the meantime, I helped them test the new weapons on those who had transformed—even Greg. I made so many suggestions to improve them..."

"That's kinda sadistic," Nancy said.

"What?" Ike asked.

Nancy scoffed. "Weren't you listening? Greg was her boyfriend."

"Ah, sorry." Ike turned to Sandy. "Yeah, that's some real fucked up shit right there."

She shot him an annoyed look before continuing. "Well, you've all seen the result of those tests. The additional training was all mind stuff." She gestured to Marty. "The serum worked, and the first time I went outside that facility I felt myself networked in with a few others, your brother being one of them."

"Wait," Marty said. "What?"

Sandy nodded. "Uh-huh."

Ike grumbled. "So, that's why they bombed our shit up?"

"Not at first. Mind you, none of that was my decision, anyway. I was nobody at that point, a recently demoted Private as I've told you. They even had an entire group of new recruits lined up for the next round of injections. But they never planned on things getting so of control."

"So, what's this about my brother?"

"I'm afraid I haven't always been so truthful about this, but once Cooley started producing cocoons, the entire facility and all the staff went on high alert status. That's around the time I discovered just how many cocoons your brother already laid. Once they learned that, they had few other options but to bomb the area, if they meant to keep the issue contained."

"What are you talking about?" Marty said, speaking louder. "I destroyed them all." He held up two fingers, then three, obviously unsure after all this time how many there had been. Already his digits faltered…

She frowned. "No, Marty. There were many more. Dozens."

Marty's face lit with surprise. "What? Where were they all?"

"Never keep all your eggs in one basket, bucko." Ike tried not to let a twisted smile appear on his face, but he couldn't help himself.

"That's right," Sandy said. "He had them everywhere. Apparently, he didn't sleep much, and boy did he keep busy. By the time he finished, he had cocoons in each of your nearest neighbors' houses."

Marty's shocked expression worsened. "But why would they—"

"He killed them, old boy," Ike said. "Saw him kill some soldiers myself. Your brother is one bad mothafucker."

"Wait?" Marty said. "You saw him? When?"

"Sorry, Marty, I should have told you sooner. No reason I

should have held that detail back, but it damn well scared the literal crapola out of me. I— I shit my pants. Really, I mean, Marty. For Christ's sake, it was downright awful."

Marty stared at Ike, perhaps wondering if this were some elaborate lie. When he didn't get what he wanted, he looked as though he were weighing his responses. Unable to find the right words to express an old pain, Marty dismissed it altogether with a wave of his hand and a sigh. Ike wasn't so sure he meant it, though.

Nancy's eyebrows rose. "Then you bombed us?"

"Yes. But know that I tried to reason with him first."

"Reason with whom?" Nancy asked.

Sandy turned to Marty, patting the air. "Jake wouldn't hear any of it. Somehow, I think my interference only made things worse. Jake went crazy, started acting unpredictable, pushing the most awful images to me. Maybe hearing those new voices in his network did it; who knows? Whatever the case, next thing you know he tried to find me."

Ike's jaw fell open. "Geeze'o hell."

"Uh-huh. You hit the nail on the head right there, Ike. That was when I discovered my ability to pull a little side stream out of the alien network. It fed off this bigger stream, but somehow, they could never detect it—unless I let them. And my ability to control that separate stream made it easy to annoy Jake and the others. I could disrupt their service."

"Incredible," Marty said.

"It's nothing," she said and punched Marty's shoulder in jest.

Ike could tell she wasn't altogether joking, though. In large, she was proud of that ability, as if ignorant to the devastation that followed. "The real cool stuff came later. You know that red line on the ceiling of the facility? That was my idea. We captured one of my side stream thoughts with a ham radio and broadcast it on his network on a loop. The signal wasn't strong enough to cover much territory, but the fact Jake could no longer hear us at all pissed him off."

Ike laughed. "Well, good."

The others were too astonished by all this. Maybe her words

even put Marty off a little, the way she kept speaking of his brother in a demeaning tone. The man had still, at one time, been his brother.

"What I did on the ship was no different, only manually. It took a while to master keeping it up all the time, but it was worth it. I near drove him crazy." She eyed Nancy with a playful smile who blushed. "Well, until the point I got bonked on the head by Nancy."

Was that what made her seem so crazy, a good whack upside the head? Ike didn't know, but he thought repeating the same word over and over for all that time would take a toll on anyone. Add in that she had been living on a spaceship, naked as a jaybird, and had to eat all that crazy shit, and maybe that accounted for all those bats in the old belfry.

"Why don't you just reestablish the interference, Sandy?" Nancy's tone sounded defensive.

"I can't."

"Can't, or won't?" Nancy asked. Tears welled in her eyes. She spat out the next part, "I— I'm sorry. It's just, Bernard…"

"Don't worry your ass none, sweetheart." Ike placed a hand on her knee.

"It's okay, Nancy. I understand." Ike believed Sandy did, too. "Have you ever been on a boat for a really long time and noticed how your legs feel all wobbly once you get off? It's kind of like that now, for me, but also… You know when you get back on, they feel goofy all over again?"

"It will take some time," Marty summarized. "But we will help you get back on that boat, Sandy."

They all nodded. Even the dog seemed to agree.

"Where did you get this dog, Marty?" Sandy said, rubbing the scruff on Bento's chin. "He's special."

"Yes, he is." Marty grinned.

"What a good boy," Sandy said. "He sure loves you."

Marty stared at Sandy for a moment then, as if she had something familiar to him. Marty laid back on his bedding, gawking at the sky. Ike did the same, scanning the clouds in the bruising sky.

"Try to rest, everyone," Marty said. "Especially you, Sandy.

We'll talk more later. For now, we need some quick rest."

A cloud drifted by, one that reminded Ike of Becca. He realized how silly that sounded afterward. No cloud could look like a woman. Sure, they were soft and tender, but...

He thought about her a little longer and decided the cloud looked like her after all. And he liked the idea it did, though he would never divulge the romantic notion to anyone else.

Chapter 37

Bento couldn't miss such a unique scent, so fresh. He lifted his head and looked for the source. There, he spotted a man running toward them. This man's scent differed from the others, distinctive from the woman beside Bento. It was a fresh scent, one that had only been there for a day or so, weak and almost undetectable.

He growled, keeping it low so as not to wake Master. He didn't want to displease Master, but a bark was crawling up in his throat so fast he couldn't contain it. Before he got the chance to release, one woman awoke.

"Bento?" the woman named Sandy whispered. She scanned the immediate area. "What's wrong?"

Bento wished he could tell her. He wanted to badly, to protect Master. Maybe he should bark.

"No, don't bark. Tell me, Bento."

His world tilted as his head went to one side. He stared at her with strange curiosity, examining her pale face, the scent emanating from her so strong. She fascinated him to the point he almost forgot about the smell of the approaching man. Could she somehow understand him? He sniffed her direction, trying to discern what could have made this possible and found nothing.

Tell me, Bento, a voice said.

The voice startled him. He leaped to his feet, scanned the area beyond the woman to check on his master, but saw no danger. He sprang to one side, then to the other side, and still saw nothing of concern. Then, he remembered the approaching man and stared long and hard in that direction. The voice hadn't come from there either.

Tell me, Bento.

There it was again. His eyes fell on the woman. She was not Master, but he liked her. She had the scent, but it differed from the bad ones. His world slanted again as he realized it was her voice he was hearing. But the words hadn't come out loud. The words were silent, in his head.

Bento sat on his haunches and studied the woman. She knew things, like how to speak his language. That made Bento like her even more. Not as much as Master, but he relished the notion he could talk to her. He turned toward the approaching man.

Man coming, he thought.

The woman heard. That made Bento happy.

Man coming. Man smells not right. Man coming, coming...near now.

She nodded and petted between his ears, where he liked it most. He was so happy she'd heard him. The reward she offered pleased him. It felt so good he almost forgot the man again. Then, seeing Master lying there, Bento sprang back to his feet, moving away from the woman's hand.

Sandy stood.

Man coming. Man coming now. Smells not right. Man coming.

Bento wagged his tail in wild uncontrolled motions. The urge to bark was so strong now, but he held it back.

"Hush now. Stay calm," she said.

Quiet Bento. I'll handle this. Now be quiet, boy.

Bento lay prone on the ground, ready to jump to action. He could hear footfalls and wanted to run at the man. Bento wanted to wake Master, but the woman had asked him to keep quiet. The need to bark was so overwhelming now, he needed release.

The woman crept forward.

Seeing this, the urge so strong, he moved with but stayed low.

Stay, boy. Stay, Bento. Wait for me. Please wait for me.

Her request worried Bento, but he tried to do as told. He

wanted to stay for the woman who could hear him. And he waited. He wanted to wait for the woman who could talk to him, but he was so worried.

Chapter 38

Marty recalled the look on her face when she first heard the faint sounds of the network again. And although this was only a dream, he couldn't keep the image of him coming so close to killing her out of his thoughts. Why had he ever thought such an act would come so easy to him? It hadn't even been easy to conjure up the nerve to draw his sword, let alone use it.

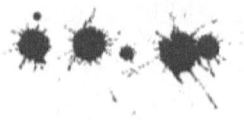

A funny thing happened to a man at moments like that, when everything was on the line. He felt helpless, knowing the fate of all humanity might lie in the crosshairs once again and that he could help. But love took over. If not for those emotions surfacing right then, maybe Sheila would be dead. That was when he realized just how much he loved her. Besides, what would he gain by her death?

Thankfully, her thoughts were elsewhere, perhaps flourishing under his brother's control for all he knew. If true, knowing that would have made it easier to end her. But even then, he didn't think he had it in him. Not yet. Maybe never. How could he harm the woman he loved?

The morning breeze teased her auburn hair. She sat in the chair atop the car, as she did many evenings. It was almost as if she was waiting to hear the network again. And lately he had found her there more often, which made it difficult to deny what could be happening.

When he stood behind her with his sword brandished, he couldn't help but reflect upon all they had been through together. Focusing on those occurrences, he thought that would somehow grant him the determination to finish what he came to do. He held that sword over her like a venomous snake for minutes, waiting to plunge its fangs deep into his unsuspecting victim's flesh. He thought her asleep.

Then, she turned her head up to him and saw fresh tears on her cheeks. She looked at him from the corner of her eye, the tears rolling down to the nape of her neck, disappearing into the fabric of her clothing. She went to speak but managed only, "I— I..."

"Shh," he said, unsure of what else he could do.

He knew what should come next. What he must do. But both knew he couldn't, that he wouldn't hurt her. Marty threw the sword aside. It landed on the ground beside the car, bouncing once, looking like a snake hiding in the grass, still eager to taste blood.

"Sheila?" he said.

"It's okay, Marty." She motioned toward the fallen sword. "We discussed this."

Marty stared at the fallen sword. When he did, the visual of what he almost did sprang to his thoughts. That alone sickened him. He had lost too much. He wouldn't allow it to come to that. If there was any other way, he would find it. And because he knew killing her would be on his mind from then on, he had to search for it alone, without Sheila.

"Marty, please." Her eyes found him.

She was so much stronger than him. He was still very much the man he had been when she met him. That was the man she had fallen for, and it was her love that defined him most. No matter how much time he spent practicing to kill her, when the time came, it would always be so much harder for a man like Marty. He cared too much about her—about this world—to take it all for granted.

He shook his head, lowering it into the crook of her neck.

She took his crown in her palms, pulling him closer, down to her breasts. He could hear her heart throbbing, how it sped up when he put his arms around her and squeezed. Something wet sprinkled his cheek, her tears mixing with his own tears. And that defined them well—they were two tears becoming one. They stayed like that for a long time, on the roof of the car, as if fate had determined their union.

She went to say something. He heard her take a deep breath and start but said nothing. She pulled him closer, hugged him tighter.

She still has hope.

No, he could never kill her.

With this realization, Marty woke from his dream.

Staring up into the blistered sky, he searched for the saucer he was certain loomed overhead. He saw none, but he heard something.

Is that Bento?

Marty sat up and scanned the landscape for the dog. He saw Bento scampering beside Sandy. She walked like a panther, stalking something together.

How odd it is for Bento to accept Sandy so easily. That dog can't stand whatever noise the network makes.

They neared their target, and something ran toward them. A man.

Chapter 39

Sandy lived for moments like this. Or, she once did. Back when she was normal. When she was stronger. Now, she doubted her prowess and worried she might not handle this on her own. The others would pay if she didn't succeed. What then?

At least she had Bento. The dog followed, even though she wished him to stay back. He kept low to the ground, so he wouldn't be so visible. They made quite the pair, two entirely different creatures, somehow connected within an invisible network. They were the precise enigma Marty's brother loathed, not because of what they were, but because of his inability to gain control over them.

The man grew closer, and Sandy slowed her breathing. She observed the manner in which he kept looking back over his shoulder, as if someone had chased him here. But no one appeared to be following the man. That didn't mean he wasn't dangerous to them, though she doubted anyone who would want to hurt them would take the time to stop and look over their shoulder so much. This man was on the run, trying to escape someone, or something.

Despite how close he came, Bento stayed low. Expecting his arrival, she did, too. She couldn't risk her deduction being wrong, and she wasn't about to fail the others.

When the man was close enough, Sandy threw herself at him, twisting her body and ramming him. She grabbed the man's arms and flung him to one side. The man staggered to a stop. Bento took hold of his pant leg and yanked, tearing the fabric, keeping the man off balance. Shocked, the man collapsed to the ground, kicking to free himself. When he did, he popped right back up and tried to flee. Sandy pushed him back down.

"Don't kill me, don't—" he said.

Bento growled at the man.

The others were awake.

Marty said, "Hold on a second. Let Sandy take care of this."

That was good because she needed this. He was a good judge of character and an even better judge of feelings.

She shoved the man back, spun him around, and mounted his back as she bent one of his legs behind him. Bento got right in his face and growled louder.

"Please, don't hurt me," the man cried.

Sandy drove her knee into his back, making it clear he should keep quiet.

"Okay, Sandy. That's enough." Marty waved the dog off. "Back Bento, back now, boy."

Bento backed off, though he continued to let out a long, low growl.

Sandy got to her feet and shoved the heel of her shoe into the man's back, pinning him against the ground. When she did, Bento went back in.

It's okay, Bento, Sandy whispered in the dog's mind.

The dog stopped growling. In a clear moment of indecisiveness, the dog looked from Marty to Sandy and back again. He sat at Sandy's feet. Unsure of what to think about that, Sandy bent and stroked the dog between the ears.

Marty saw this and grinned.

"Listen," the man said, "I only wanted to get out of that town. There's something awful back there—"

"What did you see, a fucking alien or something?" Ike asked.

The man stared at him, perhaps wondering if Ike was one of them.

Ike picked up on his unease. "Relax, I'm no damn spaceman."

The man relaxed some. Sandy removed her foot, but he stayed where he was, breathing heavy into the dirt beneath him. After a few seconds, he turned his face as if making sure it was okay and maneuvered himself to a sitting position.

Marty moved in close and knelt beside the man. "What did you see, my friend?"

A nervous smile found the man's face as he told his story.

Chapter 40

Ike listened to everything Ted had to say and tried to remain calm. It didn't surprise him to hear Jake had survived or even that he had come back. Nor did it shock him that fucker still wanted Marty, even after all they had done to oppose such a reunion. It was Ted's description of Jake that disturbed Ike.

"You're sure," Marty asked. "He was blue?"

"Not just blue, but I swear I could see right through him. And there were all these sparks shooting across his body, maybe even inside of it. Looked like tiny little fireworks."

"Holy fuck nuts," Ike said, feeling his jaw go numb.

Sandy seemed to wait on Marty's reaction. If anyone knew what sort of change Jake had gone through, she did. But he thought she knew something else, too, and he could see she wanted to tell them. The words formed on her lips before she spoke.

"It's not just him," she said.

"What do you mean?" Marty asked.

"It's all of them."

Marty's brow furrowed. "All of whom, Sandy?"

"The aliens. He's created a whole new race just like him."

Marty sighed and wiped the sweat off his forehead. Ike could tell he was worrying about Sheila.

"Whelp," Ted said, "I know nothing about any *alien race*, but I saw him bring some little creature to life. Then he *ate* it."

"What did it look like?" Nancy said.

"I'd say a rat, maybe. Only it wasn't no rat. Kinda sorta looked like a mini version of him, blue and all see through like I said. It was more like a cross between a squid and a rat, I guess, if I had to compare it to anything." Disgust filled Ted's face. "And then, he turned right back into the man, the one they're all so gung-ho over."

"Christ," Ike said, "They think he's Christ?"

Ted nodded.

Marty's face paled.

"Anything else?" Marty asked, sounding desperate. "Anything at all?"

Ted shook his head.

Ike pondered the frustration of what they learned. Jake had new powers, and not a single one of them knew just how strong those powers were or what Jake could do. Heck, Ted spoke all about the strange occurrences in town, where they all gathered around Jake, and he did his thing. Too bad he hadn't gotten close enough to describe the entire scene, but Ike had a good idea what happened. Besides, if Ted had been there, he wouldn't be here now. They would be none the wiser.

Chapter 41

Sheila stood before the Infinite, and he walked around her with purpose, observing every quality about the woman his brother loved. The Infinite didn't understand the concept of love but that other part of him still did. The shame of it all was that the Infinite would have to sacrifice this woman. Otherwise, maybe she would have made for a fine pet. She was so obedient. Unfortunate or not, the Infinite saw no other option.

He looked around, made sure no one else was around, and beckoned Bernard over. "Hold her. Tightly please."

Bernard moved behind Sheila and took held her elbows back. Sheila didn't struggle, even remained still, almost like a puppet. But it would take much more than a puppet to beat Marty. The Infinite needed an ace up his sleeve, and this woman, the one who loved his brother enough to bear his child, would be that card.

The Infinite raised his hands before her and began creating one of the special creatures. The orange illumination caught Bernard's eyes, drawing his interest. The deeper the glow, the larger the big man's eyes got. This one wasn't for Bernard, though. This very special piece of the Infinite's being was for Sheila. And it was a big part of his plan.

His hands trembled, this time not for show but because of how hard it was to bring this creature to life. It began to form, though it required something deeper from the Infinite's core before it would be ready. This was his essence, everything he was about. His arms jerked badly, struggling to maintain their placement. The thing growing between his palms stood on unfaltering hands. Complete concentration was essential to the process. Nearly exhausted, the flash came finally, and the Infinite sighed with relief. When the light faded, he held a creature in his hands the size of a rather large guinea pig, though it didn't weigh near as heavy as it looked. If he hesitated too long, it would become unstable. He didn't want it to escape, either.

Bernard's eyes widened on the creature. The Infinite was proud of his creation, so much like himself. He marveled over its translucent blue skin, watching a synapse spark before shooting through the center of the creature's body. It was already learning. If he waited any longer, he would never succeed.

"Hold her, I said."

Bernard's large hands gripped her shoulders tighter as instructed. If not for her trance-like state, she might have felt Bernard's hold on her. It would leave bruises. She still didn't struggle, just stood there waiting, willing to do whatever the Infinite desired of her.

"All right, my dear," the Infinite said in a playful tone, "Open wide, if you don't mind."

Sheila opened her mouth without question.

The Infinite stepped forward, holding his hands out. As they neared Sheila, the creature tried to free itself. The Infinite tightened his grip on the creature which began gnawing on his hand. It didn't hurt so much as it annoyed the Infinite, but he also found the act almost comical. Then he burst out laughing.

"Now, now, my pet." He brought the creature within a mere inch of Sheila's mouth. "Don't you worry."

The creature, alert to its situation, flailed about. Then, when it saw Sheila's mouth, it did what came instinctual to a creature like this and seized hold of her lips. Once the Infinite saw the creature had grasped what he wanted, he let it free.

Sheila's body shuddered as the alien creature pushed itself into her gaping mouth. The creature clung to her lips with tiny claws, its tentacles slithering across her face as it pried her jaws apart. Sheila's eyes crossed, centered on the creature. A terrified expression struck her face, and her vocal cords strained to get out the initial screams right as the creature stuffed itself into her mouth. Her muffled screams sounded wet.

"Don't worry, dear," the Infinite said. "It's all for the better good, I assure you." He believed this sentiment, too.

Soon enough his brother would be by his side. All would be well. They would rule the universe together. The Infinite would become the penultimate leader of all living and non-living matter.

Tears streamed down her face, and Sheila struggled against Bernard's grip for the first time. Bernard, no longer mesmerized by the creature, constricted his arms around her arms and chest. She kicked and stomped at his feet and shins, trying to free herself, but the big man held her in place, ignoring her futile fight. Each time she made a fuss, Bernard's grip cinched tighter.

The creature pushed past her teeth and gums, going deeper. The Jake part of the Infinite believed the creature must taste something like a giant raw oyster sliding down her throat, at least in consistency. This would test her gag reflexes. But she would breathe easier once the creature became part of her, absorbed into the tender flesh inside of her. Not in the way she was used to, though. She would be capable of breathing any atmosphere once the conversion was complete.

Gagging and coughing, Sheila relented as the creature pushed half its body down her throat. Spit foamed at sides of her mouth; her cheeks stretched to full capacity. The creature cried out, and pushed harder, straining until a third of it was down her throat. Sheila coughed, mucus flying out of her nose in a spray. Some of it landed on the Infinite's face. Dragging a single finger down his cheek, he felt the substance but didn't wipe it away. He liked how it felt, the power over this woman; it further motivated him.

The creature peered out from the depths of Sheila's throat, its beady glowing eyes focusing on the Infinite. This was the moment the creature first recognized him as its master and understood where it came from and what it needed to do. An instant later, the rest of the alien body plunged down Sheila's airway. She gagged, nearly fainting, but soon steadied as the creature became one with her. Only then did Bernard release her. Sheila left the mess of spit or tears on her face and waited for further instruction.

"Well now, isn't that something?"

This all made the Infinite happy. Content to have set his plan in motion, he laughed hysterically.

Bernard and Sheila stood unmoved, unresponsive. They were mere puppets under his control and control them he would. All of them.

Chapter 42

Marty knelt, took out the sword, and began to take it apart, laying the pieces out on the red cloth. He pulled the yellow rag from his pocket and cleaned each piece one by one, replacing them back on the red cloth when he finished. Marty remembered seeing this done by his mysterious friend Yu many times. It wasn't until much later that Yu finally explained the beautiful etching on the sword's blade.

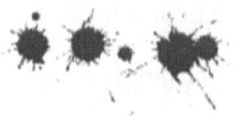

"This is the sageo." Yu removed the red silk ribbon and read the inscription to Marty as written. Marty understood none of it. Then Yu translated it for Marty, "He who is humbled by the theft this sword commits shall be enlightened."

Marty took those words to heart.

Yu showed him how to tie the sageo. He explained how to fasten the saya, or what Marty knew as a scabbard, to either the waistline or a shoulder harness. Marty found grace in the methodical manner in which Yu did this.

He released the sword, and Yu held it out in both of his hands for Marty to take. He urged Marty to repeat what he had done. Marty took great care in trying to imitate Yu's example, ashamed of his clumsy effort.

Yu grunted his disapproval.

Marty freed the sword and handed it back to Yu.

Yu knelt, laid out the red cloth and began taking the sword apart, naming the pieces as he removed them. Marty listened intently at the name of each and watched the method in which Yu cleaned the sword with diligence. Then it was Marty's turn.

He lifted the piece, wiping it with great care. "Tsuka," Marty said out loud, wiping the handle down. He picked up another piece, "Fuchi." After cleaning that, he took up another, "Habaki," each time showing the piece to Yu and naming it, waiting for his approval. Then he cleaned the piece with care before replacing it on the red cloth until he finished.

At this effort, Yu seemed pleased.

Marty reassembled the sword and handed it back to Yu. Yu took the sword, inspected Marty's handiwork, and pulled it out of the scabbard far enough to make the inscription on its blade visible.

Yu traced the engraving with admiration. "This is the mei, or signature."

His eyes glittered with tears, as if struggling to hold back emotions. Marty wished he could let it out, but Yu was not that kind of man.

"It says," Yu said, *"a good brother never draws his own blood."*

Marty's eyes welled with tears at hearing that, and he wasn't so successful at holding them back. Seeing him cry, Yu shoved the sword back into the scabbard. That was the end of today's lesson.

Remembering that day, Marty reassembled the sword as he had back then, replacing the cloth back in his pockets when finished.

He stood and perch on an old tree stump in the middle of the field, unaware if anyone back at the camp had woken yet. He had gotten far enough away he wouldn't bother them, so he could focus without distraction. A calm fell over him as he let his feelings search for the true meanings of Yu's words. With his thoughts focused, Marty took a deep breath and withdrew the sword. It rang in the sky as he thrust it outward and flicked it at the sun. He shifted his weight and thrust the sword sideways, then let it dance over his head in a full circle. It came to a hard stop mid-air, as if striking an invisible target. Marty took in a deep breath, contemplating this strike, and continued his exercises.

Chapter 43

Ike stared off at Marty.

"What's with him?" Ted asked.

Opportunities for comedy didn't come up often like the one good old Ted served up, so Ike dug right in. "He's the goddamned Karate Kid, all grown up." He snickered at his own joke while everyone else just rolled their eyes. "Come on, you were all thinking it."

"How long has he been doing that?" Sandy asked.

Ike smirked at her. "How the fuck would I know? I haven't seen him in months. When he finally came around to visit, he showed up all Kung Fu like and shit."

Sandy sighed. He knew this wasn't meant for him. They were placing an awful lot of faith in their pal, Marty. The guy who had taken up the sword just recently. Though it could be, back when Ike had lived closer to Marty, maybe he'd gone sneaking off all the damn time. Ike didn't know; he never kept a close eye on the guy. And they sure as Hell didn't spend every waking hour together. Becca had entranced Ike back then, in a horizontal sense.

Yet, we still spent a friggin' lot of the time together, didn't we?

Several hours each day, Marty taught Ike what he knew about farming. Although Ike tried to listen, his thoughts often wandered—a fact he now regretted. They must have spent four to five hours a day together. They often had lunch together. And they drank a few warm beers on special occasion, or a glass of cheap wine. Ike supposed they might have spent seven to nine hours together total on average. That still left plenty of time to their lonesome.

"I wonder if he's been swinging that thing around since back when I lived in town." Ike felt bad that his tone sounded doubtful. "Could be, for all I know."

When he looked at Sandy, he realized she knew what he was thinking, too. He wished he hadn't.

"What about the gun?" Nancy asked.

"Shit, who knows? I've never seen him shoot the damned thing, and I'm not even sure it could propel a bullet hard enough to penetrate a piece of fucking paper."

This time Nancy sighed.

Sandy surveyed camp. Her eyes found the shovel among what few items they had. Ike thought it wouldn't make a very good weapon. But it would do more damage than nothing at all.

"We need more weapons," Sandy said.

Ike nodded. He wished they still had those shock staffs from before, but he did not know where they'd ended up after the last battle.

"I'd bet my stash is still intact...you know...at my old place" Ted said. "It's not far away at all. Within walking distance even."

"Hell, we can ride there and get them," Ike said. "Be back before nightfall."

"Let's run it by Marty when he gets back," Sandy said.

They both agreed. If they planned to attack, they needed those weapons badly. Ike would feel better once they had real weapons and didn't have to rely Mr. Miyagi over yonder, on the tree stump. The thought made Ike chuckled, and he engrossed himself in preparing the meal.

Chapter 44

Nancy couldn't stand all these delays. Time slid by like a snail across a rocky terrain. And she knew, above all else, the longer they waited, the harder it would be to get Bernard back. She must make sure he was safe. And there was this nagging feeling she should hurry. Because of their hesitation, she would have to go this alone. A gun would at least serve her well, so she waited a little longer.

Even though she didn't think of Sandy as a friend, she no longer felt that deep resentment for the woman. She doubted that image of Sandy shooting Bernard would ever go away. Then again, would she and Bernard even have gotten caught up in this mess if it weren't for Sandy?

Then, there was the matter of Ike. An ambiguous and poor mannered man, he had cleaned up his act some. But Nancy still saw all the rough edges. As far as it concerned her, you couldn't trust a man like that anymore than you could a coked-up thief at a drug bust.

Between her companions and this new guy, Ted, they acted like all hell would break loose. And soon, by the sound of it. Nancy didn't want Bernard getting hurt, or, worse yet, being taken away into space like Sandy had been. She didn't want him ending up dead or transformed into some hideous monster by Marty's alien brother. And that brought her to Marty.

The guy seemed off his rocker. She couldn't tell whether he was a ninja, a cowboy, or a farmer. There he was, standing on a tree stump off on the horizon, waving his little sword around like a madman.

Doesn't that take the cake?

Marty had a gun, though. She didn't need to go to Ted So-and-So's old house to secure one. Not when she could just take the pistol Marty kept stashed away in his pouch. The quicker she got that gun and went on her way, the better.

Why not take a horse?

She could stride right into town, get Bernard, and leave without a hitch. They could make a life for themselves elsewhere, far out of the reach of the network.

What will they do when they find out? Follow me?

Then, an idea came to her, and she knew what to do to ensure they didn't.

Nancy rose to her feet, regarded Sandy, and stepped over the woman's legs as she passed. She leaned on Ike, who was just sitting there, exhibiting some trust in him. "I'm going to the bathroom," she said.

"Careful, Nancy," Sandy said, jesting and rubbing the bump on her head. "Bad things seem to happen when you take that shovel."

A laugh escaped Nancy's lips, one she thought sounded too nervous. She headed for Marty's horse, hoping before long the others would forget about her.

Chapter 45

The Infinite concentrated on an image he kept stored away in his memories for moments like this. Focus gave him the power to bring this image to reality. His translucent blue skin pulsed with sparks, traveling from synapse to synapse, nerve ending to nerve ending, producing the visual he wanted to portray. With all his energy focused on this concept, feeling like an artist of sorts, he altered his appearance save for one imperfect stroke on his canvas. This would be the stroke his brother applied to his neck.

His concentration faltered, thinking of it. He forced that memory away—for now at least—and regained focus on the image he wanted. As the sky bruised over for the night, soft pink skin started to appear over his form. It molded into the picture he thought long and hard about, as if sculpted out of clay. This was how he would secure his brother, a little trick for his brother.

Chapter 46

Sandy worried about how long it had been since Nancy left. She had taken the shovel, but it felt like an unusually long period. Even then, she should have been back by now.

She stood and walked in a wide circle around the others. Ted and Ike's eyes followed her, and she began to pace.

"What's wrong, toots?" Ike asked.

"I'm not sure."

Her eyes searched Marty off in the distance. He had started the long hike back. She wished in some ways he hadn't gone so far away.

Bento went out to greet Marty.

No longer able to stand her impatience; Sandy walked in the direction Nancy had gone. It didn't take long to realize what Nancy had done and why.

She scanned the horizon, trying to find her. "Shit!"

Marty jogged back to camp. Ike and Ted came up beside her.

"What is it?" Ike asked.

"The horses," Sandy pointed.

Ike's eyes widened on the space. "Son of a bi—"

Ted interrupted. "You think they—"

"Nope," Ike said. "That bitch took them."

Marty reached the edge of camp, his breathing steady, unfaltering. "What? What is it?"

"Fucking Nancy," Ike said. "Damn well scarfed up our horses."

Chapter 47

Times like this, Marty regretted what love did to people. Love had a funny way of making certain types of people a little twisted. Himself included. Now, love had taken Nancy and turned her into a lunatic. What did she plan to do? Ride right into the devil's lair and take Bernard with no hassle? If so, she would quickly discover just how bad of an idea that was. Hopefully that lesson wouldn't end up costing her life in exchange.

"What the fuck do we do now?" Ike asked.

Marty shook his head. He wasn't sure and still couldn't believe what she had done. Part of him wanted to go after her. Another part, the more sensible half, knew they could never catch up to her on foot. Also, going in unprepared would put them all in danger. Was he willing to sacrifice everything for just one friend?

Ike grunted. "Maybe we should go after her. Eh, old boy?"

He shook his head again, this time showing with his hand that he needed to think a minute. Pulling at the gray hairs of his beard, he hoped Ike wouldn't interrupt his thought process. Already, he was having difficulty concentrating thanks to Sandy's rampage through the camp, angered she hadn't caught on to Nancy's plan sooner. He could have spent all day reflecting on his own choices, where and when everything went wrong. But none of that really had any significance now, and Sheila had helped Marty learn how not to demonize his actions when everything went wrong a while back. He wasn't about to blame himself for this mess.

In his mind, Marty had played this whole thing out several times. Nancy had just made that all more complicated. He fully believed Sheila would be there when they attacked, standing beside his brother. It worried him what that could mean, because he knew there was a possibility it might not be the Sheila he loved anymore but some empty husk under his brother's control. That likely meant Bernard would be there, too. And now Nancy? Someone he cared for would get hurt, no doubt about it.

"Whatcha thinking about there, chief?" Ike said.

Marty was thankful for the interruption this time. Concern formed on Ike's face, but he didn't want to divulge what bothered him most. Then again, Marty might need Ike more than he hoped.

Ike's head cocked to one side. Seeing this reminded Marty of Bento when the dog was attempting to gain insight into whatever Marty pondered. Then again, Ike always knew more than he let on.

"Worried about her, eh?" Ike asked.

"Not her. Me."

Ike only stared at him with disbelief, but Marty thought he understood this conflict. No doubt he felt something similar regarding Becca. He wouldn't want to any harm to come to Becca. Ike wouldn't want any more heartbreak than Marty did, yet already he had dealt out his fair share of grief. It had affected those around him—and that was too much.

"It's why you brought me, huh?" Ike whispered.

Marty hadn't thought about this in some time, but Ike was right. His old friend was an insurance of sorts. If Marty couldn't make the hard decision, Ike would have to. That made Ike the most valuable piece on the board to Marty. He only hoped Ike would know when and what to do.

Marty nodded.

"I don't fucking envy you, brother. You know that." Ike put an arm around Marty's shoulder. "But I'm freaking here for you, man, to the end. Through the thick and thin of this shit."

Marty collapsed into Ike's arm, and, for a moment, he sensed how uncomfortable this made Ike. Then, as if accepting his role in all this, Ike hugged Marty. Ike was the closest thing Marty had to a brother nowadays.

Chapter 48

Sandy rummaged through their remaining items with angst. She needed a weapon. Sure, she might outmatch most men in a physical match, but, in her weakened state, she preferred more punch behind her words should anyone come looking for them because of Nancy going off on her own. And she fully expected someone would come. She wanted to be ready.

Would Ted fight with them of it came to that? She doubted he would, and she didn't blame him. Their odds weren't good. Marty was down his gun, so all he had was that sword, and she did not know whether he could or would use it effectively. Ike had his mouth, but no doubt he wouldn't mind a gun of some sort. Even if both somehow found weapons, she didn't like their chances. There were only three of them against all those people they saw earlier, and many more.

She considered Bento. Perhaps he could be useful. But it was more that, wasn't it? She had a feeling the dog would play a much larger role in all this. That made her consider another possibility. Could Bento have planted that thought?

She studied the dog who lay on his back, sunning his belly. His brown fur appeared almost silky smooth. He was a beautiful dog. No, he was the perfect dog. For Sandy, at least.

A quick glance revealed Ted staring at her. He made no attempt at hiding his curiosity of her, either. When he finally looked away, he watched Marty and Ike in the same manner, ignoring her altogether. The two men embraced, the sentimental nature of it all bringing back too many emotions, memories of things she no longer wanted to recall. Worrying about Greg was pointless, and even Nancy. She cared for them all too much to go through it repeatedly in her head.

Struggling to stifle any outward emotion, Sandy forced her eyes away and kicked something on the ground. Ted's eyes shot to the action. Bento startled, rising to his feet. The dog approached her with caution. Then, as if the dog somehow understood the emotional baggage that wounded her, he rubbed his muzzle against her leg.

"Aww." She really liked this dog.

Scratching Bento's head, she looked up at Ike and Marty. "All right, lover boys. Don't you think it's time we hit the road here?"

There wasn't really a road around these parts anymore. None that hadn't been overrun with thick brush. She wished there was, but those days were gone. And traveling across a thick field of brush was more daunting on foot. Unseen holes and rocks made for disruptions, a sprained ankle or the like, perhaps a few minutes to recover. She supposed they would come across a clear road eventually, but she didn't know for sure. Hopefully Ted knew of an easier path.

Ike and Marty parted and returned to the camp. Marty's face lined with tears, and he didn't bother hiding it. Even Ike's face looked a little flushed and teary. Just seeing them both like that, knowing everything they had already been through and were going through, it all made Sandy's skin prickle. Marty wiped his eyes.

"We should hurry to Ted's place," he said.

"What about Nancy?" Ted asked. Sandy wished he hadn't.

Ike grimaced; aware as she was that Nancy was lost to them.

"I believe it's too late for her," Marty confirmed

"Too late?" Ted asked. "What does that mean?"

"I'm afraid the man you saw back in town is a very dangerous man. Most of the people there are likely already under his control, if not all of them." Marty shook his head. "You were very lucky to get away."

Sandy agreed but didn't say so. She had other concerns. "Which direction, Ted? Is there a road nearby?"

He gawked at her as if having trouble understanding her.

She wondered if he hadn't heard her question, then Ted's finger swung around in a wide circle off in the distance.

"Out yonder," Ted said, "but no roads. Not really."

Sandy didn't like all the tall grass ahead of them.

"Maybe a dirt path at some point," Ted said. "If it's still there, it heads right through a farm and that's where it leaves off but might get us close."

She tried to see the path from here but couldn't. If it was out there, it must be a way away.

Marty came up beside her. "What do you think?"

As she considered his question, Ike appeared on her left. Her thoughts betrayed her, because anything she thought wasn't good. She had to weigh how much of her doubt to share with them. Bento sat at her feet. Did him being there make her feel slightly more positive about their chances? Maybe, but hope would never be as reliable as a gun.

"It's not good, I'm afraid." A cool breeze struck her neck, as if to reinforce her concern. "It's...difficult—"

Ike took Sandy's hand. His touch surprised her, but she let him lift it out in front of her. Then he did the same with Marty, until the three of them stood there, hand in hand, Bento right in the middle beneath them. It was all so touching.

"Okay," Ike said, "at the count of three we all fucking shout 'team.' Got it?"

Both her and Marty giggled.

Ike's grin widened.

Bento scratched one ear with his foot lazily.

An awkward voice behind them said something she almost couldn't make out. It was Ted, and he had said, "Team." Hearing that made her question everything all over again.

Chapter 49

Nancy doubted they would come after her. They would realize how pointless it was, that she had gotten a good head start on them, and they would give up. They would forge their own paths. As for Nancy, she had no choice but to try to get Bernard back. She had to believe this was only a temporary anomaly, that she definitely would get Bernard back, as she had last time.

Bernard had gone astray before. She had gotten him back then, but it always took time. He wasn't a strong-minded man, so it made sense someone would take advantage of him lacking a strong will. But she would get him back.

What if I get there and can't break this spell he's under?

All she needed was a chance. Maybe he was just sitting there somewhere, staring up at the stars again. If that ended up being the case, all she had to do was show up and get him on his feet. He would follow her if she showed up. But she also realized that was a best-case scenario and very unlikely.

Unlike Sandy and Marty and Ike, she wanted to consider every possibility. She had thought long and hard about what dangers lay ahead for her, what it could mean for her future if she ended up being wrong about Bernard. But life without him wasn't a life worth living, so she had to try. Besides, she wasn't sure she belonged in Marty's little group without Bernard at her side. She never was close to Marty. She didn't really even care what happened to Ike or Sandy. What else did she have left for her back there? That new guy, Ted? Or perhaps the dog—

What was his name? Bento?

No, none of them mattered to her as long as Bernard was missing. It was unfortunate she had to make the trip alone, but she had made many trips on her own long ago. She had visited France, Spain, and Mexico—all in one summer even. How was this any different?

She could be a strong woman when the circumstances required her to be one. If nothing else, she had determination. Once she set her sights on something, she would see it through to the end. That was the precise way she felt about her relationship with Bernard. She loved him, and she *had* to get him back.

Despite the late hour, everyone was still out and about as she rode into town. She saw him right away, standing next to a fire. Beside him, she saw Sheila of all people. Had found each other through this mess? Maybe he was still okay.

She dismounted the horse fifty away. Many people noticed her, but none—not even Tia—offered any greeting. Their blank stares tracked her progress to Bernard.

There was a time when Nancy thought she had made the wrong decision. It all felt so...off. Identifying with this fear, she drew the gun from her waistband and brandished it in her left hand for all to see. The gun felt weird there. A rifle would have been better; although Nancy didn't like guns, she had used a rifle as a teenager enough she could fire one with confidence. But guns had such a sense of finality about them. All it took was the slight twitch of a finger. A gun could take life with such ease, leaving a person for dead in a fraction of a second.

There was also something to be said for how having the gun made her feel. It wasn't the power. Not for a woman like Nancy. She had all the power she needed just by being part of Bernard's life. No, it was sin. Being bad like this gave her an unexpected thrill.

Growing up in Southern Illinois, her parents raised her as a strict Southern Baptist. While she rebelled against the ideals of religion her entire youth, she always abided by God's law. Now, here she was with this gun, and oh my, there was something about it she kind of liked. Perhaps that sensation made her feel so weird about the gun. The notion she could take someone's life kind of even turned her on in a strange, demented way. If

Bernard was gone, would she have the strength to pull that trigger? She thought maybe she could, but she would have to be certain.

Nancy closed in on Bernard, but he didn't seem to see her. Sheila saw Nancy first, acknowledging her with a slight smile. Perhaps, her odd expression was in part because of the gun. A weapon always created unease, even between friends. Then another thought struck her.

What if he's grown tired of me? What's Sheila even doing here?

Would Bernard leave her for Sheila? They did share that stupid cosmic bond. She recalled how Bernard and Sandy had been communicating without speaking, so it made sense he and Sheila had the same capability.

Then it occurred to her that having a gun in hand was feeling right. Bernard looked at Nancy, and what she saw on his face wasn't happiness. The expression he held for her wasn't one of surprise or even joy, but complacency. He didn't appear to think anything of Nancy's arrival. Could something like that spark a love interest? She did not know, but she'd be damned if she would allow any woman to get between her and Bernard.

At ten yards away, Sheila approached Nancy, beckoning for Bernard to follow. It was to deny the power Sheila had over him, and that made Nancy's neck feel like it was on fire. And that sensation spread around to her cheeks a bowl of warm water.

"Why are you here, Sheila?"

Sheila didn't answer.

"You should be back at home where Marty left you."

Again, Sheila didn't respond.

"You don't belong here," Bernard said.

"Hush now," Sheila said.

"What's going on here?" Tears stung at Nancy's eyes. "How dare you say such a thing, Bernard? Are you saying...that you— Are you leaving me for this...*tramp*?"

Nancy's finger dangled out in front, casting an accusatory glare in Sheila's direction. The stoic Sheila remained unfazed by Nancy's allegations. But Bernard's gaze went from Nancy's outstretched finger to Sheila to Nancy and back again. He nodded, although she did not know what he was agreeing to, but she thought he was speaking of infidelity.

Tears flowed hot against her cheeks, down her neck, feeling like thin ice cracking. She had expected nothing like this. Here was her man with Marty's woman, and they were together, and neither of them were denying anything.

Marty would be just as upset.

She aimed the gun at Sheila. Unmoved by the gesture, Sheila didn't seem to see Nancy as any threat. To make matters worse, Sheila even turned away from Nancy, as if to snub her. Sheila put all of her attention into Bernard, whispering something to him Nancy couldn't hear.

Bernard moved on Nancy. "Give me that gun."

"Why did you do this, Bernard?" Nancy asked.

"I need that gun." He came within a few yards from her. "Give me the gun." His tone sounded loud and hateful.

"I can't—" Nancy said.

Bernard came close enough she could smell him. He elbowed her cheek, and she nearly fell. But he was on her fast, trying to pry the gun out of her hands. A welt swelled upon her cheekbone. She ignored the pain, focusing on maintaining a hold on the gun. She wasn't about to let Bernard have it, let alone Sheila. The report echoed across the field as the gun recoiled into her gut. It felt like Bernard had punched her, but she didn't think that was what had happened. Blood soaked into her shirt. Panicked, she felt for a bullet hole but found nothing. Because she hadn't shot herself.

Nancy's eyes rose to Bernard's. Then they went down his stomach and saw all the blood spreading across the fabric of his clothes, a hole in the center. He didn't cry or scream or anything, only stepped forward and pried the gun from Nancy's trembling hands.

He extended the gun, lowering its barrel to Nancy's chest. Without hesitation, Bernard pulled the trigger. It felt like cold steel piercing her chest, followed by the hottest sensation she ever experienced. Falling to the ground, she struggled to get to all fours. Unable to maintain the position, she dropped and curled up like a baby.

Sheila came up beside her. "You will be okay."

Something about the woman's voice sounded unreal, in part because of the deafening sound of the gunfire. Already the pain was numbing her, the feeling of cold death taking a firm grasp on her soul, pulling her to the afterlife. She saw a flash of light.

"Quick." Sheila's voice sounded distorted, not her own. "Eat this."

The thing in Sheila's hands was blue, a mushroom-like food. Nancy grabbed for it but failed. Sheila held it to Nancy's mouth, assisting her in chewing and swallowing by working her jaws for her. A beautiful glow emanated from Nancy's chest. The pain faded. As it did, a single word popped into Nancy's thoughts like a lion pouncing on a gazelle.

"Now."

Darkness followed.

Chapter 50

A s they walked, Marty's thoughts went back to his time training with Yu. He thought about Yu's note to him, the last words he would ever receive from the man. If there were anyone else left in this world that Marty considered a brother—other than Ike—it was Yu. He had given Marty strength in a time when he had felt weak. Yu helped bring focus to a troubled mind. Marty owed the man a great debt of gratitude, and he had tried to pay that deficit through brotherhood.

Marty sat at Yu's kitchen table. The lifestyle the man chose impressed him. There was no bed. Instead, a heavy quilt lay sprawled out in one corner of the office-building floor. Yu had rigged an old wood-burning stove into the side of the building, which allowed the man to overlook the cityscape from the sixth floor while he cooked food. How he had ever gotten the thing up this high was beyond Marty.

Yu got up from the rustic picnic table and went to the stove. He stirred the beans, taking a moment to warm his hands over the pot before returning to Marty.

Marty had noticed a change in Yu recently, and that concerned him. The man had closed himself off to Marty emotionally. Their dealings were becoming more of a business deal than a friendship, and that bothered Marty.

Trying to break the ice, Marty said, "You don't quite seem yourself these days."

Yu peered across the table at Marty, appearing guarded of Marty's query. He stood, walked back to the beans, and ignored the question.

"I worry—"

"Stop there," Yu said, warning Marty with a hand gesture.

"But, Yu—"

"I don't want to talk about this, Marty." Yu stirred the beans. He sniffed and appeared satisfied by the aroma. "The food is ready."

Yu filled two bowls with a ladle full of beans and placed a spoon in each. Returning to the table, he slid one bowl across to Marty with a brief smile. Yu sat and lifted his spoon, then let it fall as if the utensil had suddenly taken on an immense weight.

"I killed my brother," Yu said.

This statement froze Marty. He to console Yu, to say all the right words to soothe his friend. He could barely speak at all, though, and what came out was a jumbled mess. "Yu... I—didn't know. I'm—"

"Hush," Yu said. He sat the spoon in his bowl and pushed the food away, his hunger taking a back seat to obvious sadness. "The worst part is, here I am on the eve of the third anniversary of his death, and I'm helping you prepare to kill your own brother."

"He isn't my brother anymore."

"Isn't he? Won't he always be your brother so long as a single drop of his human blood remains?" He gazed at the finger he had struck at Marty and withdrew his hand sheepishly. "Sorry."

"It's okay. Besides, it isn't like that, and you know it." Having lost his own appetite, Marty also pushed his beans aside. "He isn't my brother. Not anymore. You are more of a brother to me than him now."

Yu studied Marty with careful eyes, as if searching for the truth. Marty suspected he found it, as Marty had intended the words as a dagger, meant to appeal to something deep within the man. Yu seized his beans and ate fast. Marty only watched, realizing he hadn't been too hungry anyway. The more he observed Yu's nature though, the more he became aware how much Marty's plan to end Jake affected Yu.

Whatever past Yu had, it continued to trouble the man. Marty wanted to help ease that sadness, to talk things out, but Yu remained a closed door on the subject. That left Marty with many questions, and, when he left that day, he had this sinking feeling it would be the last time he saw his friend. He hadn't wanted to feed this belief, but something inside of Marty nagged at him throughout the night.

When Marty returned the next day, Yu was gone. He had left behind the sword along with the two cloths. Beneath them, Marty found a note. Even as Marty read the note for the first time, he cried.

Dear Marty,

I consider you my brother, so I will offer you this advice in parting. My brother was also a monster. If I hadn't struck him down, he might have killed many more innocent people. I, too, had no choice on the matter. But I assure you, not a day goes by where the realization of what I've done doesn't haunt me. What if I could have saved him? What if I could have fixed everything? Maybe my brother and I could have shared some final words to ensure my brother forgave me in his passing. It has been a blight upon my soul, a curse that I alone must bear, much as striking down your brother will unveil your truth. Use the sword as you intend, but never forget mei.

Best,

Yu

Those words stayed with Marty throughout the day, while he trained, and all the way back home. Even when he went to bed that night, he considered them, what Yu was really saying, how defeated the man sounded. Would that also be Marty's fate?

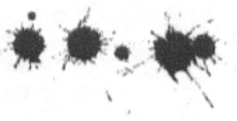

Marty felt fresh pinches on his cheeks as he recalled that last word, the play on words. He had to work to hide them from the others, while they walked to Ted's house. He had been successful. Whenever Marty thought about what he planned to do, he couldn't help but worry about the consequences of such actions. At the moment, though, he saw no other way to make things right.

Chapter 51

The Infinite sat in complete darkness, considering all that had transpired. Perhaps he had underestimated his brother. Why would Marty send Nancy alone? Was she a mere decoy? When had Marty become so good at these sorts of distractions? Then again, why hadn't Marty's attack come directly after her arrival? That would be how the Infinite handled the matter.

Perhaps the Infinite had delayed the inevitable for too long. Had he dragged this out? Maybe he should take the fight to Marty. The Infinite hadn't needed the others to handle this woman for him. She had been easy to deal with, requiring only Bernard and maybe not even him. She was such a weak woman, so it made little sense why Marty would send her.

Unless he didn't.

The Infinite considered this. That was possible. Or maybe Marty had sent an expendable pawn, meant to throw the Infinite off-guard, to make him overthink everything. What exactly was Marty's game here?

He had this growing urgency to finish this conflict. Mostly because he loathed the way he felt about Marty. The Infinite wanted the comfort of being himself again, aboard his ship, where he commanded all. Why postpone this any longer than he had to?

Greed washed over him. He rather liked the idea of ending this before it got complicated. The Infinite had everything he needed to end this foray.

Okay, so, how best to employ these minions?

He thought long and hard on the matter and pushed a single

thought into every meat bag he no longer required. He kept only those few essential to his cause nearby, and mostly just in case something went wrong. He pushed a thought to find his brother, his brother's friends, and for his people to bring them here for the Infinite to deal with. As he pushed the thought, a feeling of immense satisfaction overcame him as he discovered his brother's group were approaching the house Ted claimed was his own.

The end is near.

Chapter 52

Ike looked from Sandy to Marty. Yep, there he was crying again. Marty tried to hide it, but Ike saw it all the same. It made Ike feel bad for his old friend. Hell, it was tearing Ike up inside, but he wasn't sure of what he could do to ease Marty's concerns other than be there for the guy. He wondered if Sandy saw it, too.

Sandy was much colder than Ike remembered. No doubt some of that came from her extended stay on the S.S. Outer Fucking Spaceship, but she would have time to search her thoughts and feelings, to dwell on her regrets, once this mess was behind them. Sure, she had been alone, frigging naked, and, for Christ's sake, eating God only knew what shit she found on the ground, but she was a strong woman. But was she still a strong woman?

Trying not to worry about it, Ike observed Ted. The guy seemed too fucking content for all this, much more so than Ike suspected a man would be after the hell he claimed to have witnessed. Good old Ted never faltered at a single suggestion they had made, and that was the reason Ike didn't trust Ted. Perhaps the man wasn't as guilt free as they once believed.

Ike scanned the dog who didn't appear bothered by the man at all. That dog had a way of sniffing out creeps like Jake, a fact that Ike was thankful for once he got wind that was what was going on with the mangy mutt. If it hadn't been for that attribute, Ike wouldn't have given the dog a second thought. But, now he did, with great consideration, too.

Nothing.

Now Sandy looked at Ted, too.

Is she picking something up from that mutt?

She glanced at Ike, perhaps wondering how much he knew. Ike shrugged, though he wasn't sure how she would perceive the gesture. Sure, he sensed something all right—this guy Ted was frigging weird. And that rubbed Ike the wrong way and then some.

"Soooo," Ike said. "What's your dealio there, Ted?"

Ted looked unsure of Ike's words.

"You know," Ike said. "What makes you tick, man? I mean, are you in this for the shits and giggles or something more?"

Ted still looked confused. "I'm not sure I'm grasping what you're asking, Ike."

Sandy grinned. He liked her smile. She could be pleasant when she wanted to. Despite their little back and forth, Marty kept to himself, probably trying to wipe away his tears without them seeing.

"Well, you're just full of surprises, is all. 'Cause it beats the frigging hell out of me why your so gung ho 'bout our little plan. I mean, you just met us."

Ted came to an abrupt stop, and everyone else did the same. The man looked as though Ike had struck a nerve. "The house, it's just up ahead. We're close." He spoke to Marty. "We can talk more there, but let's get to safety."

Ike tapped his foot, his patience being tested. Frigging Ted offered nothing more. When Ted started walking again, they followed, but Sandy and Marty were smiling as much as Ike. They both knew what Ike was up to.

"What the fuck is waiting there for us at that house, Ted?" Ike asked.

Chapter 53

Any other day or situation, the way Ike acted might repulse Sandy. Perhaps that was the reason why their connection had never been a strong one. But there were rare moments when there was something almost magical about Ike, the way he could throw someone off-guard, to say something they hadn't wanted to. When Ike was in his game, no one in his crosshairs stood a chance.

Ted faltered. "I'm not sure what you mean."

Marty approached Ted.

Sandy saw slight discolorations on his cheeks. She hadn't cried in so very long and for good reason. Tears came with sadness. Sadness brought memories. Memories brought Greg. None of that would make this any easier.

Marty patted Ted's shoulder. "I believe he's asking why this is so easy for you to go along with, Ted. It's a fair question."

"Thanks, Marty." Ike folded his arms across his chest. "Seems good old Ted got a fucking frog crammed in his throat."

Ted wrinkled his forehead. "I told you, I'm no—"

Chapter 54

Ted did not know what they wanted from him. Yes, he had secrets. But why should he share any of that? He didn't even know who these people were, having just met them.

He had escaped. They all knew that. But he didn't want them to know that those people hunted him down. He didn't want to talk about how they restrained him, or the thing they forced him to swallow. Ted couldn't bear to think about what had happened, yet still the memories came.

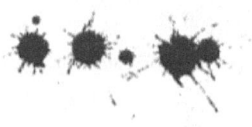

"Hold him!" the stranger said.

Several of Ted's fellow townspeople clung to his arms, keeping him upright, his entire weight supported by his arms alone. The stranger stood before him. Ted expected the man to wail on him for the intrusion, but he didn't.

"Bernard," the man said, "help him to steadier feet, please."

The large man made his way behind Ted. He struggled to see what Bernard was doing. Then Bernard stuck his arms under each of Ted's armpits and lifted Ted into the air. Once he was against Bernard's broad chest, some others let go, but a few stayed to make sure Ted couldn't free himself.

"Hold him tight," the stranger said.

He held his hands out in front of Ted. An amber-colored glow spread between his palms, and Ted considered the stranger might turn into his other self. Maybe that was all the man had in store for Ted, to let him know he was in control. At least Ted hoped it would be that easy.

The man's hands were putting off some warmth, especially as they glowed brighter. Neither hand trembled though they appeared to go through strain. A bright flash burned onto Ted's eyes, and he struggled to see anything. In that instant, Ted was so scared he would have believed anything just to get out of this, even that the stranger was the very person he claimed to be. Maybe he was their savior, too, as he had performed miracles. Although the glow in his retinas hadn't fully faded, he saw the thing in the stranger's hands and that gave perspective to everything. At first, he believed it was some giant slug, but it had limbs like an octopus. Only its head was almost rodent-like with ferocious looking teeth. Whatever it was, it was not of this Earth, and it wasn't heavenly.

"What the—" Ted said. "Get that thing away from me!"

He screamed and couldn't keep himself from sounding like a young boy, one that hadn't reached puberty yet. But Ted wanted to stop, to keep his mouth shut. Only he couldn't. His thoughts focused on his every worry and then some. Was this creature going to eat him alive?

As if to confirm that suspicion, the creature's rat-like teeth chattered. A small spark of energy shot from the creature's bulbous head down its extremities. The man kept a firm grip on it, even when the creature began gnawing away at his finger. But the man's wounds healed as fast as they appeared.

"Tighter, my dear Bernard."

The man came closer. When he did, Ted screamed. More so when the stranger brought the creature up to his face.

"No! Not my face!"

It was so close now. Ted could hear tiny sounds, little pops and clicks as it noted Ted's presence. The stranger nodded to someone—Tia. She walked up to Ted and placed her hands on his cheeks. Despite his fight, she pressed her thumbs into the corners of his mouth and forced his jaws wide, shoving her forefingers into his upper palate. Now, when Ted screamed, his tongue darted in and around her fingers, trying in desperation to push them away. Though he could no longer see what was happening, he felt everything. Something slimy touched his tongue. What was it?

The creature...

No, it couldn't be. Yet, try as he might to deny it, he knew the truth. The creature wasn't trying to eat Ted. It was trying to find the way in, deep inside of Ted.

It thrust itself into Ted's mouth and down his throat, forcing bile up on all sides. He felt the burn on his tonsils. Trails of spit gathered at the corners of his mouth and ran down his chin, and finally Tia let go as the creature stuffed its entire self into Ted's mouth. Tears strained at Ted's eyes, afraid and in pain. He didn't know what to do, how to escape, or even if he could.

The creature shoved itself down past his Adam's apple, and Ted could no longer breathe. His eyes strained on all these people, seeing them one at a time, trying to recognize them so he could beg for help. No one helped though. They all just watched.

With one final push, the creature entered him fully. When it did, the air came back to him. He sucked in air, let it out fast, over and over. For several minutes, his mind swam, and he thought he could feel the creature moving around inside of him, not in his belly, but as part of him. It had unrestricted access, and the thought sickened him. He gagged, then dry heaved, and tried to bring the creature back up. But it didn't come.

The stranger lifted his hands in the air as if praising the moment. When he lowered them, they let Ted go. Ted ran without hesitation, a chorus of laughter behind him. That laughter haunted him for miles, but they never followed him. They let him escape. But why?

Returning to the present, Ted heard Ike's question. "What the fuck is waiting there for us at that house, Ted?"

"I'm not sure what you mean." And he didn't either. How could he? He wasn't one of them.

"I believe he's asking why this is so easy for you to go along with, Ted. It's a fair question."

"Thanks Marty." Ike folded his arms across his chest. "Seems good old Ted got a fucking frog crammed in his throat."

Ted wrinkled his forehead. "I told you, I'm no—"

Then Ted heard another voice, one deep within himself. That voice said only one word.

Now.

Chapter 55

The first thing Marty noticed was that Bento was having a fit, whimpering and squealing. Seconds later, the dog was howling at Ted. Ted seemed oblivious to the entire scene.

"—alien," Ted finished.

Marty wasn't so sure. Judging from Ike and Sandy's expressions, he wasn't alone, either. This was so much bigger than he thought, wasn't it? Ted could serve as a homing beacon for the others. Marty couldn't bear to think what might happen if his brother attacked them, instead of the other way around like he had planned.

"Oh no, you sure aren't, Ted." Ike raised an eyebrow to Marty, and although Marty saw it, so did Ted. And Ted looked suspicious of them all.

Marty folded his arms and took a bold stance. It was ironic he should do this so soon after bawling his eyes out. But he didn't want to stay under such a critical thumb, eternally internalizing his own shortcomings. Marty had to focus now on whether Ted could be trusted. He thought not. But how could he communicate that to the others without Ted suspecting anything? Marty had an idea.

"Ted," he said, "how far is the house?"

Both Ike and Sandy looked a little shocked. That drew Ted's attention, too. He studied all of them. Something about Ted's inquisitive gaze cautioned Marty that he should try to be more aware than ever.

"You sure there, mate?" Ike ran a hand back through his rough hair, which Marty believed a show of doubt. That echoed Marty's concerns.

"Maybe we should head back," Sandy said.

That would be the safest thing to do. But it was unlike Sandy to retreat, and, although he knew she was right, it didn't mean that was what they would do. Marty considered their opinions, and Sandy's appealed to his immediate fears. That wouldn't serve their purpose, though. It was far too late to run, anyway. A plan began to form in Marty's thoughts, albeit it one that wasn't thought out. But it would be.

"I really think we *should* check out Ted's place, for guns and food." He wanted them to know he was on to something, but he didn't want to reveal too much to Ted. Who was he kidding? He knew Jake was in there, hiding behind Ted's eyes.

Sandy and Ike nodded, though reluctantly. Ted did, too, appearing as though his head dangled from an invisible string. It made Marty sad to witness this level of control, as it reminded him of Bernard.

Is this how Sheila will act when I see her next?

The thought of it made him sick. He couldn't bear seeing her like that, a mere puppet to his brother. He hoped whatever Jake did to make them this way didn't hurt. Most of all, he hoped he could bring her back from it. That she could become her old self.

Marty's gaze fell on Ike. His eyes said, *Not a fucking chance, old boy.*

He realized Ike might be correct, too. That this might be the precise case and the very reason he had wanted Ike to tag along on this journey. Without him around for the blow-by-blow, Marty might make the wrong choice when the time came. That could lead to an even bigger mess. He needed someone to reveal the hard truth, and who better than Ike? Considering what might result, Marty tried to conjure up all the ill thoughts, feelings, and emotions he held for his brother and redirect them at a mental image of Sheila.

It didn't work. He couldn't imagine feeling the same way about her as he did that *monster*. It would be too personal, so close to home. She knew things about Marty even Jake didn't have a clue about. That alone could account for Marty's downfall if he wasn't careful.

"So," Ted said, breaking Marty out of the trance-like state. "We going or what?"

"Oh sure, old boy," Ike said. "Sure, we are."

Ted grinned.

Ike returned the gesture, then turned away from Ted. He made a quick universal motion for a blowjob. Sandy saw this and burst out in laughter. Ted appeared oblivious to Ike's kidding, and knowing Jake was so out of the loop on all this made Marty laugh. When he did, Ted reciprocated for no obvious reason. His laughter was cold and monotone, out of place. Just hearing it sucked all the jocularity out of the moment.

Marty placed a hand across Ted's shoulders, reinforcing the concept of newfound friendship. Overall, they needed Jake to trust them. He also needed to ask a few questions of Ted—not Jake but the real Ted—and he couldn't risk sounding too offensive. Nor did he want to make Jake suspicious. Above all, his new plan relied on something he hadn't in a very long time: faith.

"Do you have a fireplace at your house?"

Ted examined Marty, deep in thought. This was Jake searching Ted's memories. "Yes."

"Perfect. We should start a fire once we arrive. Okay?" Marty looked at Sandy. "I wish there was a way we could check in on some of our old friends." He hoped he wasn't being too obvious. "I'd like to make sure they're all okay. You know, keep the lines of communication open between us."

"Oh, fuck yeah," Ike said, grasping what Marty wanted. "I've been worrying about Miss Daisy for a frigging coon's age."

Sandy didn't appear to understand at first. Then, as if suddenly grasping what he wanted, she spun away from them. The action caught their eyes—even Ted. But try as he might to comprehend what Sandy was doing, Jake seemed unaware. When Sandy turned back around, she wore a large smile. Marty had his answer. Now, all that remained was to see his plan through and hope it all came together.

Chapter 56

There was a time when Sandy worried her gift had somehow been severed from her. Would she never connect to the network again? Wouldn't that be a good thing? Who could want to remain part of that or any other network? Then, comprehending the need for it now, to disrupt the bigger network again, Sandy had to work just to tune it in. Upon hearing them again, she couldn't help but smile.

Like a candle in a light breeze, the network wavered at first, like the difference between a flicker or light and a full out blaze. She heard Jake's attempt at mocking what she had done back on the ship. Its purpose was similar: to hide something from them. Over and over the word repeated itself.

Infinite. Infinite. Infinite. Infinite.

This only made her laugh harder. It had been her idea, yet here it was being used against her. But he wouldn't be able to shut her out forever. Her training alone made her an intimidating adversary. If not that, the ride ahead might be a very bumpy one. But she was certain she could succeed, so she flashed Marty and Ike a big smile. They appeared to receive this as intended.

They approached the house in silence. Sandy was grateful for this. Already she was looking for a hole in Jake's network. Jake was a tricky one, but, when it came to will of mind, she had the upper hand. There had to be a way in. She would find it and exploit it.

A large white colonial house sat in the distance, nearly untouched by the past devastation. Why would Ted have ever left such a place? Several small trees lined the backyard, but the grounds were flat and rather ordinary. She could tell the house was long abandoned, so they wouldn't have any trouble getting in.

"Ike, why don't you give me a hand gathering up some firewood?" Marty said upon reaching the front yard. "We have to stay warm."

Ted smiled as Marty turned to him.

"Ted, you and Sandy see if you can rustle up some grub. We'll be in shortly."

Ted led the way and Sandy trailed him. She shot Marty a wink. Bento trotted beside her.

Seeing this, she thought hard. *Go to your Master, Bento.*

Bento remained by her side.

The dog had latched onto her. Although that made her happy, there was no time for joy now, and there might not be time for it later if he didn't go to Marty.

She tried again to push the thought again. *Go to Marty, Bento.*

Bento's head tilted, interpreting the command best he could. Then he turned, watching Marty head toward the back of the house. Marty whistled, but the dog remained.

Go now, Bento, Sandy suggested.

Bento looked up to her for a moment, then ran to catch up to Marty.

Chapter 57

Ike struggled to keep pace with Marty, who took bold, heavy steps toward the backyard. All the while, Marty kept glancing back, what Ike surmised was him making sure the dog followed. The dog caught up, and Marty placed a hand on Ike's shoulder, steering him toward a dense patch of brush.

"What's the plan, Boss?" Ike asked.

"Well, it won't be easy."

"When is it ever frigging easy?"

Marty chortled. "That's a fair point." He kneeled before the dog and scratched the fur between the dog's ears. "We need to get out of here and fast. I suspect Jake's people are coming for us. Sandy will fend them off best she can for as long as possible."

"Sounds like fun. We've been walking for hours, why the hell not walk more?" Ike choked back his laughed when Marty indicated it might be too loud. "I tell you I'll be one cut mother after this is over."

To this, Marty grinned weakly.

Ike knew what that meant. That was Marty's way of telling Ike to shut the fuck up, yet still acknowledging it had been funny. Sensing this, Ike kept quiet and waited to hear the plan.

"Bento?" Marty said. The dog scooted its hindquarters closer, looking anxious. "Bento, I need you to listen. Can you do that?"

The dog looked left, distracted by a rabbit. A twitch came to the dog's hips, as if he desired to give chase. The moment passed.

Marty stroked the dog's fur. "It's important, Bento."

Ike sighed. "This is your frigging plan? Have a chat with a goddamned nut-licking mutt?"

"Ike, please."

He hushed, but doubt seized Ike's thoughts like a python. Was Marty trying to communicate with this dog? Was that the plan? It was absurd. No, it was more than absurd. It was crazy.

"Bento, you need to help Sandy."

The dog turned its head up to Marty quick as lightning. It had recognized her name. Was it coincidence? Ike didn't know.

"You have a gift, Bento," Marty said, "and I need you to *help* Sandy."

The dog bowed, its gaze on Marty.

"Help Sandy, Bento. Together, you can do it. Help Sandy... and protect her."

The dog made a quiet crying noise. Ike didn't know what to make of it. Was it possible the mangy creature understood Marty or did the noise mean something different, like an invitation to scratch the dog's ass? Maybe the only thing the dog was anxious about was to get busy needling his balls with that hairy nose of his.

Marty reached for the gun. "Blast. I forgot."

Nancy had taken the gun. Ike was sure he meant to sneak it to Sandy, but he also thought Sandy was smart enough to have secured some other weapon by now, something inside the house. That would have been one of the first things she thought of, for sure.

Marty patted the dog between the ears. "Ike and I have to go, Bento. Take care of Sandy. Keep Sandy safe. Help Sandy. But remember, she needs to wait, Bento. She has to wait until the last second." Marty said a silent little prayer. "Now, go. Help Sandy."

Bento remained for a second, as if trying to digest Marty's commands. Then, the chocolate Lab took off running for the front door of the house. Ike couldn't believe it. When it got there, Marty heard the telltale barking, as Bento begged for someone to let him in. Moments later the barking stopped.

If they didn't skedaddle right quick, Ted would come looking for them. Or maybe someone else would. If there was a mob coming, Ike felt bad for leaving Sandy on her own. There had been so many of them passing their camp. Now, there would likely be even more of them. Sandy was in no condition to take them on by her lonesome. At least she had that mutt to help her.

Not that that's any better. Ike sighed.

Ike refocused his attention on Marty. "We need to go, big guy."

Marty nodded and got to his feet. They started off behind the tree line, moving swiftly away from the house, back in the direction from which they had come. Ike hoped they were far enough out of view that no one could see them from the house.

"You think that dog will do a goddamned thing?"

Marty nodded.

"What makes you so sure of this, Zorro? That furry mutt is as much of an eating, pooping factory as any other dog."

"He's no ordinary dog."

"Looks plain Jane enough to me, El Capitan."

Marty pulled Ike in closer as they walked, making sure he identified a large tree branch somewhat hidden by the knee-high brush. "Watch where you walk." Marty grinned, appearing rather calm considering everything. "You know, I didn't just happen upon Bento. I went searching for him."

"So what? Big freaking whoop. You wanted a chocolate Lab. All sorts of fucking people want this dog or that dog."

Marty chuckled. "Ike, did you ever notice how nobody has a dog anymore? Or even a cat?"

Ike considered this. He thought hard about what it could mean but came up empty. He had seen horses, cows, and goats. But not a single cat or dog. Except for Bento. "Fucking A...no, I haven't." Ike's tone had a certain sense of wonderment to it.

"Well, I went looking for them. And I know they weren't all there, but there were a lot from this area, and they were all there with Bento."

"Geezo Christ! What was he to them, their leader?"

"I don't know for sure. Maybe Sandy does, but I look at it like this. We have our Sandy, and I think Bento might be their equivalent, or maybe something along those lines. Who knows the how or why, only that it appears true. Does that make sense to you?"

Ike tried to make the comparisons but struggled. All this talk was pure speculation. Maybe people just didn't see any use for pets in the wake of the alien apocalypse. Maybe dogs and cats didn't need people, either. Their instincts would take over.

Ike dismissed the conversation. "So, what's our part in all this?"

"Well, my friend, I think when the time comes, we will have a small window to strike."

Ike scoffed. This plan was pathetic. "You think all these things—the moon, sun, and stars—are going to fucking align for us like good little boys and girls?" There, he said it. He had tried to curtail his words, but now that it was out in the open, Marty had to address it. Still, massive guilt washed over Ike, and he felt his cheeks blush.

"I found something I lost, and it assures me we will be okay."

"Something has definitely changed about you." Ike smirked and jabbed a finger at the ponytail. He wanted to twirl a finger around one ear as well but thought better of it. "Okay, so, what the fuck is it already?"

"Faith, Ike. I found faith."

Sick twisted knots seized Ike's stomach. It churned before Marty finished getting the words out. He took in the ponytail, the sword, and Marty's strange grin. He wanted to throw up.

"We're fucked," Ike said.

Marty laughed, but Ike noticed something about Marty right then. He had swagger again, confidence. Somehow Marty had assured himself they were to succeed. Ike was sure it wouldn't end well, and Marty's confidence could be the very attribute that cemented that failure. With that sinking feeling in his stomach worsening, Ike forced his thoughts to Becca. Was she okay? Though he didn't know, he hoped so, and he couldn't wait to see her again. He longed for an end to this, and that far exceeded anything else. But there was also something to all of this Ike hadn't foreseen. Ike felt an obligation. To a friend. To Marty. To his brother.

Chapter 58

What some might see as Marty getting his insanity back, others still might see as cockiness. Marty knew what it really was, though: faith in shining brilliance all over his soul. It was difficult to deny. Because of that, the very ground they ran on no longer smelled like a plain old field. The smell was stimulating, fragrant trees with light teased through their leaves, all of it so refreshing, inspiring. A new era of prosperity was rolling in; Marty was certain of it.

Sandy would disrupt the network. He would finish Jake off this time. He saw only success in their future. And, when everything was heading in the right direction, Ike yanked him down to the ground by the collar of his shirt.

"Ike, what the—"

"Shush, fool."

Ike's finger traced the line on the horizon, leading back toward the house. Marty saw movement.

"Look at all those shits out there," Ike said.

Droves of people headed for the house. It relieved him to see that of his plan had worked.

"This isn't good, Marty."

He didn't see Ike's point. They had gone where he wanted them to go. Then it occurred to Marty, they had to get to Jake and fast, and they would never make it in time on foot, unless they ran full speed for a very long time. Sandy wouldn't be able to hold them off forever, and if the two of them couldn't get to Jake in time, all would be for naught. Sure, he still had his faith, but it no longer felt so reassuring.

Marty tried not to think about, focusing on staying low and crawling as fast as he could across the landscape. Ike trailed him by a few feet. When they reached a point where the twilight hours of night hid them, they leaped back to their feet and took off running. Already Ike breathed heavy as they ran toward their destiny, toward whatever faith would offer them this time. They ran toward Jake.

Chapter 59

Sandy rummaged through the kitchen pantry as fast as she could. She found soup cans, canned peaches, some corn, and many other non-perishables. None of it what she needed.

Ted pushed his way past her, and ducked into the pantry, scanning what was available. "We can cook beans over the fire. Beans are good."

He removed two cans of kidney beans and walked over to another cabinet, searching for a pot. As expected, he didn't seem to know where anything was in this house. That confirmed her suspicion that this wasn't his house. Knowing this only hastened her search for a weapon.

Sandy closed the pantry. She wasn't sure what she hoped she would find there, anyway. People didn't keep guns in the pantry, not usually. She hoped there was something more daunting than a kitchen knife.

"We'll need a can opener," she said.

Ted glanced from drawer to drawer before directing her to one next to the stove. As she moved to it, his unsure expression seemed to intensify. She hoped to find something menacing there, but part of her knew she wouldn't. Dishtowels were all she found there, but the mistake didn't even faze Ted, who was busy looking elsewhere. Seeing him doing his own rummaging, she moved to the next drawer without a word and found many plastic and wooden utensils there. Among them was a can opener.

She picked up the can opener with a sigh. That was when she refocused on the set of knives in a large block of wood, sitting on the counter. All the big knives, the ones that could maim someone, were missing. A few steak knives remained, so, careful not to be seen, she slipped one out and slid it into her pocket.

Better than nothing, she supposed.

A dog barked. She placed the can opener on the counter and started for the front door. "I'll be right back. Have to let Bento in."

As she left the kitchen, she noticed Ted's odd smile. She knew what this meant. Ted was no longer in there. Whatever was—likely Jake—had been amicable to nearly every suggestion. It was creepy and made Sandy uneasy, but she hid the emotion well.

Bento sat outside the door, barking. She opened it, and a small whine escaped the dog as he scampered inside. While there, Sandy scanned the horizon and spotted several tiny silhouettes, far off in the distance, all of them approaching the house.

It's starting already.

She had to prepare but doing so without Ted noticing would be difficult. She needed to be quick.

Bento?

The dog ignored her. Part of this might be because of Ted, but all those people outside were likely driving him crazy. And Jake's interference no doubt distracted him. It must have sounded like a thunderstorm of words pouring into the poor dog's head.

Bento?

This time the dog came and sat before her.

What did Marty tell you, Bento?

The dog appeared to consider the question. Sandy didn't think he would understand everything she had said but hoped he would comprehend enough. Then again, knowing how special this dog was, she wondered just how much he had understood about everything that already had and was continuing to happen.

Help Sandy. Help Sandy. The dog's tail wagged. *Protect Sandy. Yes, good Bento.*

This relieved Sandy. She hoped Marty and Ike and were far enough away that Ted couldn't see them. Even if he did, she wasn't sure he would notice them among all the others. Either way, he would figure it out eventually—especially if all those people outside spotted her friends—so she would need to deal with Ted soon. And she would need to take care of those others. But Ted was the endpoint all the others focused on, what was drawing them in.

Wait, Sandy, Bento said. *Wait. And help Sandy.*

This last bit needed careful consideration. She doubted Bento had picked up the entire message, but hearing this last bit, she knew the dog had captured the most important parts. It was clear that Sandy needed to *wait* before she tried to disrupt the network again. Judging by how close those others were, she wouldn't be able to wait long, but she would do so as long as possible.

She bent over and gave the dog a nice scratch on the cheek. Bento looked as though he was smiling. He turned his muzzle up to meet her eyes.

Love Sandy.

This shocked Sandy. The notion of unconditional love like this took her by surprise, and that brought her back to reality. She realized she felt the same way about this dog.

Love Bento, she said back.

Bento spun and lowered his muzzle, tail raised, and growled. There, standing in front of Bento, was Ted. Bento's ears went back. Sandy almost told Bento to relax, but Ted had startled her.

"Did you say something, Sandy?" Ted asked.

She knew what Ted likely heard. Love had a funny way of lowering one's defenses. She had let her guard down, and Ted had heard a voice all too familiar to him in the network. Not to Ted per se, but to the other man—or rather the creature on the other side of the network. Jake.

Chapter 60

The Infinite preferred solitude. He left Sheila and Bernard outside to keep watch while he rested. Although he didn't require respite, part of him desired the privacy. He also wanted to focus on Marty and his little group of friends.

This last occurrence was a peculiar one? When he heard the thought, there was something familiar about that tone. More so, the words surprised him. Had he heard this woman say, *Love Bento*?

When he moved Ted into the room, the woman seemed guarded. And that dog started growling, as if it had somehow seen him through Ted's eyes. Could the dog see through the Infinite's meat bag skin suit?

The Infinite studied the dog through Ted's eyes, trying to read its thoughts. What little he picked up made little sense. Either the dog had abilities beyond what the Infinite could understand, or this woman was covering up the dog's thoughts. It had to be the latter.

"Say," the Infinite asked through Ted, "Where are our good friends, Marty and Ike?"

He was well aware how that sounded. Sarcasm was something he loved about the human languages. He supposed it existed in every dialect throughout the cosmos, but humans were so good at it. He maneuvered Ted to the door, hoping to glimpse Marty and Ike, so he could see what they were up to. When he did, someone moved behind him.

The Infinite spun, expecting to see the woman, only to have the dog surprise him. The creature was leaping at Ted, his jowls drawn back in a ferocious snarl. He tried to withdraw the large butcher knife he had hidden from Sandy and stuck in his beltline but couldn't get it out in time. He batted the dog away with Ted's forearm. Bento struck the wall with a yelp, rolled into an immediate attack position, and came again.

Sandy had a steak knife she thrust at Ted. He sidestepped her and spun Ted's body out of harm's way, but she was fast. He felt the cool sting of the serrated blade in the back of Ted's left leg. The Infinite winced, feeling every bit of that blade but determined not to lose control of Ted. The dog bit his pant leg and tugged hard.

The Infinite dug in his waistline for the blade, got it out but not in time to defend himself. The dog bit Ted's arm, its teeth deep in the flesh. The pain was so great he dropped the blade. The knife rattled across the hardwood floor and struck the baseboard.

Losing the weapon infuriated the Infinite. He pushed for his people to assault the house now. He wanted them to take revenge. Sitting there in complete darkness, he pushed the thought over and over. The darkness was essential, especially in this temporary form he had chosen. He couldn't stand seeing himself like this until he had no other choice.

It won't be long now.

Soon, he would gain control over Marty, and he would leave this planet. He would take his people and his brother and leave this forsaken place.

He pushed a thought to instruct Sheila and Bernard of his wishes should Marty show up. Either way, all was in place for the Infinite's success. Until that moment came, if it ever did, he could let this little game play out without too much intrusion. That meant he could remain in the dark, the only place on this Earth he felt comfortable at the moment, in this skin.

Suddenly, he realized Ted was in pain. He stifled it best he could, but a growing inability to concentrate plagued him. Even when the woman moved in behind Ted, he had already conceded to lose the battle, to sacrifice Ted. If he lived, maybe Ted could be useful at a later time, if need be.

The Infinite winced as he felt the blade in the small of Ted's back. While the Infinite was trying to remove the knife, Sandy mounted Ted's back, withdrew the blade, and prepared to strike again. When she plunged the knife in his shoulder, Ted collapsed. The dog came at Ted, and the Infinite used Ted's arms to fend off the feverish attacks. One arm was almost useless to the Infinite, the muscle likely severed, so he mostly fended off the dog with one now bloodied hand. It was time to abandon this meat bag.

As the Infinite left Ted's body, he glimpsed the knife being withdrawn from Ted's shoulder. He saw the shadow cast against the wall, displaying another attack with that knife. The blade struck the base of Ted's neck right as the Infinite left. Again, there was darkness.

Chapter 61

Sandy left Ted to bleed out in one corner of the room and started working to barricade the door, the windows, and any other means of entering this house. Though mind controlled, these people and Jake would have enough intelligence to problem solve. They might even equip themselves with tools or weapons. If that ended up being the case, any barricade she put up wouldn't last for long. Knowing this effort would only slow them down, she didn't want to invest too much time in securing the home. But she needed enough time that she could start the disruption again. And that very much could mean she would end up dead if they got to her before then.

Not that she feared death. She had carried a great burden for so long, her role in Greg's death. If her dying somehow made them even, then so be it. Besides, she had taken a quick survey of the rest of this house and had found no guns. Even if there were some, she no longer had the time to find them. Nor could she hold back all those people armed only with a dog and a couple knives. Unless they saw her coming at them and died of laughter.

Sandy kneeled and tried to slow her heart rate. Each time she tried to calm herself, her head ached. The wound hadn't enough time to heal, and she struggled to keep the spider webs of pain from ruling her thoughts. In her mind, she saw the energy drifting with purpose among images of her past, her daydreams. She attempted to grasp hold of the cloud of conscious thoughts, but it slipped through her mental grasp. Sandy tried again but faltered once more.

As she worked to regain control of her subconscious, her thoughts wavered, unable to zero in on what she needed. Then, in her mind, she saw Bento.

She opened her eyes. The dog was staring at her. Did he know what she wanted to do? Could he help? And even if Bento could help, was it possible for Marty to get there in time and bring an end to this madness?

Help Sandy, Bento said.

Yes, Sandy thought. *Good Bento*.

Turmoil came from all directions as Bento and she worked together. A window broke. Someone was trying to pry the door open. Wood split. Someone crawled across the floor. She forced all these noises to the background and reached for the cloud again. This time, she took hold of it with her mental grasp, and, with Bento's help, worked fast to disrupt the network.

Chapter 62

Marty thought they were lucky to have found the bike. They must have looked ridiculous, two grown men riding an old, disheveled bike down a stretch of road that ran parallel to Bernard's village. Finding that road had been fortunate. Jake would be there waiting for them in town, and, with luck, they would defeat him, too.

No, not luck. Fate.

When the road curved away from the town, they abandoned the bike and ran for the village. This was part of the reason Bernard's townspeople had chosen the location, as it wasn't easily accessible to would-be pillagers and thieves.

On the way, Marty thought of Sheila. For so long he had been preparing himself for the inevitable. Now, as they made their final approach, he realized that time had come. Would Ike ensure he made the right choice? Was that too much to put on his friend's shoulders? Guilt overwhelmed him.

Several steps behind him, Ike struggled to keep up. In the short distance they had traveled, Ike had stopped to take several very short breaks. With Ike being so out of shape, he was gasping for air most of the way, and Marty worried his old friend would soon faint if they didn't stop soon. But there was no time for that now, not with Sandy in danger.

They came within sight of the camp. Marty spotted Bernard first. It was good to see him. Nancy came up beside Bernard and stood in front of him with her arms spread wide, as if defending the big guy.

As he got closer, the man Marty had waited so long to see

again appeared. Jake looked as he had in his heyday, back when he was healthiest. The shock of seeing his brother like this was one Marty hadn't expected. It sent his memories into a tailspin, remembering all those games they played as kids, all they had been through together, what they had suffered.

Then Marty saw his gun. Jake had it aimed at his friends. When the time came to strike, Marty would have to be fast. Any hesitation, straying from his plans at all, could mean they would die. Everything had to fall into place without a seed of doubt. Only then, when Marty realized how mad this was, did his faith falter.

What am I thinking?

Here he had set everything in motion, and it all depended upon luck and timing? A sick feeling twisted in his gut. Now Marty needed to catch his breath.

"Wha... What is it?" Ike stopped, bent over, panting heavily but trying to keep his voice low.

"What have I done?" Marty whispered.

Ike shook his head. He hacked something up and spat a large, brownish wad into the grass.

"I've set my entire plan into motion based on faith. On *faith*, damn it."

He twisted away from Ike, tugging at the hairs of his gray beard. There had to be some other way. Must be.

Chapter 63

"Aw, fuck," Ike said in a low tone. "Goddamn this shit."
"I know, I know." Marty patted the air, signifying they both needed to keep their voice down.

Marty took a few steps away, but Ike followed, thinking Marty had misunderstood.

"No, you old fuck." Ike put his arm around Marty's shoulder, using him like a crutch. He hacked up another wad of phlegm and tried to speak quietly. "I wouldn't have come with if I didn't have some faith in you, brother."

"Faith? In me?"

Guys like Marty never understood how great they were. Ike could see Marty's frustration, all the worry. Only good men worried about others at a time like this?

"Hell, Marty. You think the last time we did this shit, it wasn't all based on faith? You think everything went according to plan, but that plan was all about faith. You don't think we were damn lucky bastards back then? And you don't think some higher power smiled a little on us shits, instead of letting a flow of godly urine sprinkle sunshine on our asses?"

Marty's tension eased.

"We got goddamned lucky," Ike continued, "and don't you ever freaking forget that. And why do you think I followed you into that shit hole of a hive? It was faith my man. I placed my faith in you then, and I'll damn well place my faith in you now. You're a good bet."

"Ike, I don't—"

"Fuck that shit. We're doing this. You need to get your

fucking game face on and do this shit now. I have faith in you."

Ike shoved Marty in the chest playfully.

"Come on, get your little sword ready."

Marty wavered a moment, then appeared to shake out of his daze. That was it. They were all in. The bets were all on the long shots.

Chapter 64

When they took to running again, Marty ran silent, a trick Yu had taught him. Behind him, Ike's clumsy, heavy footfalls and heavy breathing worried him. If Ike kept struggling to bring in enough oxygen to keep running like this, Jake might see them coming. Marty couldn't risk it. And Ike would be of no use to Marty if he couldn't breathe. Marty made his first choice, and it was a difficult one.

Marty slid one leg out and tripped up Ike. His old friend face-planted on the ground, hacking and coughing, trying to catch his breath and stay quiet all at once. Marty continued on.

Now there was another problem, though. Where Jake was standing, Marty couldn't get a clean swipe at his neck. He would have to go for the body and hope there would be time—confusion even—to sever the head afterwards.

He scanned the area for Sheila but didn't see her anywhere. He worried what that could mean, what things Jake might have done to her to bend Marty's will. He tried not to contemplate this, but the thoughts kept springing to his mind like popcorn popping. In that moment, Marty felt more alone than he ever had before. He regretted leaving Ike behind. Now, he would have to make the hard choices all on his own. And, if Sheila got in the way, he would have to do the one thing he had been long avoiding.

Chapter 65

Ike struggled to get up to all fours. There he caught his breath, trying to stay as quiet as possible. Once he felt somewhat better, he got to his feet and looked for Marty. It fascinated him how fast and quiet the old man moved. Hell, it was damn amazing for a man of Marty's age. He watched in awe.

Ike had known from the moment he showed up at their house, that Marty was in far better shape than him. But he hadn't thought the gap between them this large. Knowing that now, it made sense for Marty to go on alone, but he would have rather Marty told him that then tripped him up like that. Regardless of his wounded pride, Ike knew the consequences of Marty's decision. That meant Ike didn't have much time to recover and get back in the action.

He hacked into his shoulder, trying to stifle the sound. When the coughing stopped and his vision steadied, Ike started walking.

Ike saw Bernard and Nancy, but they didn't see him. He saw what he thought was blood on Nancy's shirt. Their expressions were off, seemingly out of place for their situation, which began to unfold before Ike as he got closer. Jake stood in a threatening pose in front of the two, a gun aimed at Nancy.

Concern rushed over him. Ike didn't like this one frigging bit.

Something was wrong with this scene. It was too easy, and everyone was out in the open. For Christ's sake, neither Bernard nor Nancy was putting up a fight. Why wasn't Jake freaking out? Holding a gun on them wasn't exactly a big threat either.

What about some bodily harm? Why in hell weren't they all doing something, anything?

The answer came to him right as Marty burst into the air, his sword out to his side, ready to strike.

It's a trap.

Yes, it was. Wouldn't Jake have predicted this?

Ike yelled, "Marty—"

But it was too late.

The blade found flesh and drove through Jake's stomach. Marty's brother spun to receive the blade, almost as if he had expected and wanted this to happen. Marty hit the ground and quickly rolled on top of the fallen Jake, withdrawing the blade from Jake's belly.

Marty got to his feet so fast, sword raised. Ike had only a second to envy the ability. Marty prepared to strike Jake's neck.

"Stop!" Ike screamed through strained lungs. "Stop, Marty!"

Chapter 66

His people pounded on the door. Windows broke. An arm poked through one window. The Infinite peered through Ted's weakening gaze. He saw the woman he loathed, and her little dog, too. They were working together.

He clawed at the floor, moving Ted's body toward the fallen knife. Ted's fingernails snapped, broke free of the quick. Blood trickled out, making the laborious chore more difficult. With each scoot closer to the knife, Ted waned. The flesh surrounding the nail was tearing away. The Infinite used those gnarled fingertips to dig and scrape and pull Ted closer to the weapon.

Reaching out, he grasped the handle. That gave him a renewed surge of energy. The Infinite pushed Ted's body beyond its limits, pulling him up to his knees. Ted faltered, eyes blinking uncontrollably, his vision appearing as though Ted had gone underwater. Then, Ted's vision cleared, and the Infinite saw the woman and dog again.

Just a little longer.

The blade dragged across the wooden floor. It wasn't loud enough to break this woman's concentration, or the dog's. Regardless, their feeble attempt to infiltrate his network would end. He had allowed it by accident once before, so he felt determined not to let it happen again.

Ted slipped and landed face first on the floor. He lost his grip on the blade, sending it across the floor to Bento. The dog didn't stir.

The Infinite lifted Ted's head, forced the man up to elbows up, and from there tried to scoot Ted's body to the knife. The flesh of Ted's elbows quickly bruised and scraped. So long as there was still breath in Ted's lungs, the Infinite would use the man. Ted had lost so much blood, and his legs began to twitch. Ted's left arm remained a hindrance, so the Infinite put all the weight on the other and dragged Ted onward, until he secured the knife again. This time, he held the blade in his right hand, the good one, ignoring the bone sticking out of the fingertip. He clawed over to Sandy and pulled himself back up to his knees, readying to attack her from behind.

Sandy remained unmoved, still trying to wriggle her way into his network. The Infinite forced Ted to lift his torso until he was in a praying position. Then he thrust back Ted's good arm, knife in hand.

Bento's bark started the Infinite—then another noise directly outside the shack in which he sat in darkness. Things were going exactly as planned.

The Infinite wrestled Ted's body, wanting him to strike Sandy down now. He tried to force the arm forward, seeing the dog pull out of its trance. With Ted's body withering away, the Infinite sent everything he had through the meat bag and forced the blade on its path. Before he knew the result, Ted was gone, and the Infinite forced out.

Chapter 67

Marty heard Ike, but Marty didn't want to, not until he finished. He lifted his blade, preparing to land the fatal blow. Jake didn't struggle or put up any fight, something Marty hadn't expected. Blood seeped from Jake's shirt to the dirt, where it clumped. Marty had expected something else, maybe a dark green slime-like blood like last time.

"Stop, Marty!" Ike said.

Then another voice came through, faint but audible.

Now, Sandy said in his head.

She did it, had broken through. But it wasn't fully clear until he heard Bento's howl alongside her voice, streaming through his head.

He refocused on Jake, seeing his brother's deception for only a second. Beneath him, her red hair in tangles, lay Sheila. She clutched her belly, the pain resulting from his blade obvious in her expression. Then the vision was gone, as the disruption went away.

Something moved behind Marty. He spun around and saw another Sheila, one untouched by his sword, exiting the shanty. Sandy and Bento's disruption returned, and the unscathed Sheila transformed into the one person Marty feared most.

Chapter 68

Hearing her voice again in *his* network pissed him off. The Infinite got to his feet and exited the comfort of the darkness. He had done so in time to see Marty mid-air, striking the very person the Infinite had planned for him to attack. The wound wasn't near as severe as he would prefer, but it was there all the same. Marty had killed the woman he loved. The Infinite was thankful for his abilities.

Isn't that splendid?

Turning his attention back to the disruption, they had spoiled his moment. He had thought Ted had ended their effort but evidently that meat bag had failed even then. Now, the Infinite found it difficult to maintain a hold on anyone. And before he could do anything about it, he lost the only two people he had around to protect him from Marty's wrath. With both Bernard and Nancy useless to him, he needed to think quick.

The Infinite extended his hands, and an orange glow formed between them. Then he recalled the gun, saw it just lying there on the ground, close enough to grab.

He retrieved the gun and fired.

Chapter 69

The two gunshots froze Ike momentarily. He sped to the scene, hoping he wasn't too late. There, he found Marty, his sword readying to strike. Ike assumed the unfamiliar monster standing there was Jake. Marty's brother ignored Ike and focused on Marty. Jake held the gun, and Ike was certain he'd shot Marty. But Bernard and Nancy stood hand in hand, blood dripping from their stomachs. Both of them dropped to the ground at once.

"Hey, fuck face!" Ike said.

"Fuck me?" Jake turned the gun on Ike. When he did, Marty made his move.

Thank God for pony-tailed ninjas.

Chapter 70

Marty flicked his blade at Jake. The blade took the hand in which Jake held the gun. A purplish blood sprayed from the wound which already appeared to be forming a new hand. Now Marty made his final move. He brought the sword up and brought it down into what he thought was Jake's neck, hoping to reopen the old wound.

Jake staggered away, clawing at the sword stuck in his body as he bobbed along the wall of the shanty. Marty worried the cut hadn't been deep enough, but only stood there watching as his brother struggled to stay afoot. Then, Jake flickered. He didn't only flicker, but the image of his true alien self replaced the Jake that Marty remembered best. Seeing this, Marty was no longer sure of anything. He once thought everything he had known of Jake was gone. Was this some part of his brother shining through?

Again, Jake flickered. He stumbled back, nearly collapsing the shanty's wall this time. Only then did Marty realize the alien form was smiling. From what he could tell, they were two separate entities.

Marty went to Sheila. He fell to his knees beside her, the strength leaving them all at once.

Jake pulled the sword from his translucent body, opening the wound further, and tossed it aside. The Jake form came again, this time long enough to reveal Marty's strike had been a good one. He shifted again, the translucent flesh glowing a brilliant, bright blue. An orange flash came from somewhere deep inside the alien form, shooting across the body like a falling star. The blue light flickered, but still the Jake monster laughed.

At its neck, strands of translucent flesh tried to mend the wound, again and again. Each time it couldn't complete the task, the image slipped to the Jake that Marty remembered. Flickering back and forth, the body landed close to Sheila's failing body.

She looked up at Marty with weak eyes. He saw happiness in them; glad he finally found the strength to do the right thing. What she didn't see was that he had failed her. Failed his wife.

Bernard and Nancy slumped over one another. Barely hanging on, Nancy pulled herself close to Bernard's. He was already dead. She grabbed his hand and held it close to her heart, and she died there hand in hand.

Marty had failed them, too.

"Please!" Marty turned to Jake, his face hot and flustered. "If there is any part of you in there Jake, help me. Please."

The creature lifted his alien body and rested a moment. When its voice came, it surprised Marty how well it could speak, even now. "Oh, that'd be fine, Marty. And whom shall I save first? Your friends? Your woman, perhaps? Or how about your child?"

Alien Jake laughed boisterously.

Marty hadn't known. Hearing the truth now, his anger overflowed. He felt cheated. Fate had taken advantage of him once again. He had lost everything all over again. Tears streamed down his face as he lifted Sheila's head with care.

"Why, Sheila?" But he already knew why. She had known he would never do the right thing if he knew about the baby. And she was right.

Marty turned his attention back to the creature, pleading to a man he no longer believed existed. "Please, Jake!"

Again, came the sarcastic alien laughter. "Oh, dear brother, I'm sorry, but Jake's no long—" The alien life form froze.

"Mar...ty?" a fragile voice said.

Marty stared at the creature, seeing the tendrils of flesh still trying to heal over. Given enough time, the creature might succeed. Maybe it was stalling.

"Marty?" When it came the second time, he heard that

mid-western twang and knew this was his brother.

"Jake?" Marty said, flabbergasted.

The creature lifted a trembling hand, its body fall to one side, as it pulled itself closer to Sheila. The fingers rose over her stomach, and Marty let it happen. The digits glowed, and pulses of electricity sparked in the creature's head, working their way down its arm to the hand. The sparks gathered there, taking on an ominous glow. The hand settled on Sheila's stomach, and, in an instant, she took a deep breath, as if she were trying to breathe for the very first time.

When the hand fell away, Marty could see the freshly healed flesh beneath the remains of her torn and bloodied blouse. Sheila convulsed in his arms, and he worried it might have all been too late. He couldn't break free of the fear of losing her. She coughed violently, and a thick puddle of black sludge trailed down her cheek and instantly dissolved into dust.

"And my child, Jakey?" Marty's voice wavered. "What about my child?"

The alien body struggled, the tendrils starting to mend the neck back together. "I...I—" His brother's voice struggled. "Lo... ove y...you."

In the next half of a second, the head rose back to place, the tendrils of skin formed fast, repairing themselves. The creature quickly regained control. It rose to its knees over them, Marty stunned by how fast it all happened. Worse yet, the creature was laughing even louder now.

Chapter 71

Now Ike knew why he was there. It had been brewing up inside of him for some time, like boiling water. The heat of it swelled on his cheeks. He saw the creature rise to its knees, and he bent to retrieve the discarded blade. It surprised him how light it felt in his hands. The balance was magnificent.

Ike took a bold step forward, lifting the blade high above his head, trying to emulate what he had seen Marty do on the tree stump. He brought it down quick, before anything else could happen. It felt too easy.

Chapter 72

Silence. Complete and utter silence.

Sandy rejoiced. Even Bento seemed to notice the sudden peace.

Sandy moved a desk away from the window, wanting to see how those outside were doing. Dark clouds rolled in over them. She listened, but didn't hear any thunder, only screams as she realized a bad storm had arrived.

She jumped to her feet, shrugging off Ted's corpse. Running to the front door, she moved the furniture out of the way with purpose. Once she had freed herself, she stepped out on the porch, only to realize she was too late.

One by one, they ascended upward into the storm clouds, screaming out for help that couldn't be given. There was concern they might come for her, or even Bento, but they didn't want the ones they couldn't control. That meant they were safe but knowing that didn't make any of this easier to watch.

Chapter 73

Marty stood over the alien corpse. Whatever had infected Jake long ago seemed to have somehow purged itself of Jake's body. With nowhere else to go, it lay in a pool beside his brother, where it, too, would die.

The bile struggled to find another suitable host, but they all stepped away. It was too weak to come after them. The bile withered upon itself. Marty watched as it saturated the soil, trying to use even the dirt as a host. Marty smiled as the bile dissolved into the ground, finally cast out from this Earth.

To be concluded in:
RECKONING
Book Three of the Infinite Cycle

Good Brother

The boat swayed over a swell and everyone below, including Yu Swyi, panicked. He didn't know if the authorities had discovered them, as few were successful sneaking into America.

"Stop all the fidgeting," his brother Kaito said.

Kaito had learned English from books and taught Yu when they were still young. While their parents never took to it, the boys had planned to venture to the United States their entire lives. Now that the time had come, Yu worried they'd gone about it all wrong. Even if they didn't get them while on the boat, eventually they'd catch up to them in the streets or at a job, wherever—because ICE never stopped looking. So many others who ended up being deported after a lengthy stay in the States without a proper visa had informed Yu what would happen. If only they'd done this right, maybe he wouldn't be so worried.

Despite it all, Yu steeled his nerves, not wanting to show any weakness in front of his brother. Kaito always had been the stronger one, the leader. He was the sole reason Yu had come along, because the man had a way about him that attracted people to follow. Yu was merely Kaito's brother, a nobody, a regular guy with no special skills. Without Kaito, Yu would feel lost.

Yu stared out through a portal in the hull. "I don't see anyone. You think we're caught?"

"Don't know. But if you don't hush, we'll get caught for sure, loudmouth."

Yu whispered, "It's just that, I don't see any boats. I think it's something else. Did you hear that rumble? Thunder maybe."

"It isn't even raining, Yu. Besides, how you gonna see any boats when it's this dark out? Lightning, sure. But you won't see any boats unless they have their lights on. And if they're out here trying to catch us, they might not put them on until the last minute."

"You know, if it rained a few miles away; we would hear the thunder even this far away."

The rumble came again.

"See?" Yu said, staring at the dagger tattoo on his brother's arm. "You hear that? Sounds just like—"

"That wasn't thunder." Kaito looked ill. "It's bombs."

"What? Bombs? Why would they—"

But he didn't have to ask. Kaito knew what bombs sounded like, had even witnessed the bombings of entire cities in his travels. He'd hidden in bunkers below the surface, in alleyways with walls tumbling down around him. Kaito had seen enough to know where he wanted to go and why, and that's how he chose the U.S., because no one ever bombed the States. Not for a long time, anyway.

Until now.

"Listen." Kaito pulled him close. "Those are several miles inland. But if they come any closer, we're gonna need to bail. Understand?"

Yu nodded.

"I can't have you standing around not knowing what to do when the time comes, got it?"

Yu nodded again.

All these years later and Yu still felt like a young boy when his brother talked to him. Yet here he was, well into his thirties, and not a single effort to free himself of that burden. He'd depended upon his brother, to lead the way, guide them through the tough times, which were plentiful. Even now, Yu waited patiently for his brother's word, anxious and yet mindful, certain the time would come.

But that moment never came, and soon they docked along a shore filled with bristly bushes and other underbrush. Tall trees dotted the inland area, thick as a dog's fur. Yu did not know how they would get anywhere. Were they to go through the woods? Walk around them? Apparently, it didn't matter to the men who owned the boat, because as soon as all seven of them gathered their belongings and got off the boat, they pulled up anchor and set off along the coast, heading elsewhere.

The moon glowed large in the sky, surrounded by billowing gray clouds in a pitch-black sky. Yu could hear little, other than the sounds of the wake crashing on the shore. He felt the sand between his toes. It reminded him of Miyako Island. They'd gone there when he was still young, but he remembered the sensation well enough to recall how it felt. A wave of sadness fell over him at the realization they'd left their parents behind with only a letter to inform them of where they'd gone. He wished they'd done more, said more, even said goodbye. Already, he missed them.

"Put your shoes back on," Kaito said. "We need to head through those trees until we reach our contact."

Yu obeyed his brother, and they set out walking through the dense forest of pine trees. This wasn't exactly what he'd pictured when they spoke of New Jersey, and before long, that became clear when they reached the town where they were to meet their contact and all they found was ruin.

"Not much to look at," Yu said.

"This can't be right." Kaito stared at the tiny self-made map. He studied it, tracing their route with his finger. "This is all supposed to be—well… Not in shambles."

"You think this was what we heard? The bombing?"

"Nah. Look around. This is old news. Whatever we heard earlier, that's farther south." Kaito put his hands on his hips. "Well, I don't see anyone." The other five defectors had gone their own way. "I think maybe we find someplace to hole up for the night. We head west in the morning."

Kaito kicked through rubbish, making his way toward one of the few buildings still standing. When they got there, he threw open the door, and Yu followed him, shutting the door before he took in their surroundings.

"What is this place?" Yu asked.

"A convenience store. Not much to eat. Looks picked through. Whatever happened here, it was recent." Kaito looked left then right. "Spread out. Let's see if we can find some supplies and something to eat."

Yu headed down one aisle, Kaito the next. They kept pace with each other, stopping here and there to examine things they'd found. So far, Yu had found a Whatchamacallit candy bar, a small bottle of shampoo, and a bottle of peach schnapps someone had stashed behind the register. He wasn't much of a drinker but supposed, given their situation, they deserved to celebrate. It wasn't every day you got away with sneaking into America.

Thinking about it now, everything felt too easy. Where had the Coast Guard been? Surely someone patrolled the beaches. In fact, where was everyone? He hadn't spotted a single soul yet, dead or alive.

"Hey," Yu said, making his way to his brother. "Where do you think everyone went?"

"No idea. My guess is with that bombing being so close, they evacuated to a nearby town. We will head out in the morning, and I bet we find our contact in the next town over. It's probably something minor."

"I've never thought of bombing anything as a minor situation."

"Yeah, well, get used to it. This is America, baby! Land of the free. Home of things that go boom. They love to blow shit up here."

They both laughed, and although Yu knew his brother was only kidding, he wondered if there might be a sliver of truth to that statement. Perhaps the contact information Kaito had was too old, and they'd cleared the area for bomb testing. That would make sense. But, if that were the case, why was there still all these supplies lying around? And it had looked freshly picked through. In fact, the dates on what few snacks they had found all signified most of it was still within its use by date.

"Listen," Kaito said. "Tomorrow. If we *do* see someone, make sure you speak their language. If you don't do that much, they'll never listen to a word you say. Especially our contact. Got it?"

Yu nodded.

"Now, you gonna pass that schnapps or what?"

They drank into the wee hours of night, both sloshed by the

time they'd drank two-thirds of the bottle. After they finished it, they both fell asleep, Yu struggling to stay awake longer than Kaito and failing.

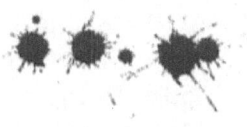

Yu woke before daylight, ready to set out west. Right away he noticed his brother missing and went looking for him, only to find him kneeling just outside the front door, cleaning a sword. Yu opened the door.

"Is that grandfather's sword?"

"Yes," Kaito said. "You remember what he taught us?"

"How could I forget?"

Kaito looked at Yu sternly. "Make sure you don't forget." He finished assembling the sword, folded the red and yellow cloths, then stood, sword in hand. "I saw a being earlier."

"Really? Who?"

"Not a who but a what..."

Yu felt a wrinkle form on his brow. "What do you mean?"

"Whatever it was, it wasn't human. Maybe they once were—I don't know. Whatever the case, this *thing* flew in and came right for me."

"Are you okay? What happened?"

"Grandfather's sword, that's what happened."

"You killed it?"

"Yes. Left its corpse right over..." Kaito stared off on the horizon. "There, somewhere."

They walked together, Yu feeling somewhat anxious as they neared the place where Kaito had killed a monster. Only, when they got there, while the evidence suggested a struggle that led to blood loss, there was nobody.

"I don't get it," Kaito said. "I killed it. I'm certain of it."

Yu scanned the perimeter. "I think it's best we get out of here. Whatever attacked you might still be out there."

They gathered their meager belongings and headed west, hoping to reach another town soon. But it wasn't until nightfall they saw much of anything, as a dingy motel came into view. Without a word, they headed for the shelter, needing some rest.

The motel was cleaner than it looked from a distance, perhaps its weathered look the result of the bombing. A thick coat of dirt and grime covered the exterior, but the rooms were clean enough and even had running water...for now. Yu took room #2 and Kaito room #3. After they'd both showered, they met in the courtyard.

"Hey, want some of this?" Kaito said.

Yu looked at the bottle. "What is it?"

"Don't know. Someone left it in my room. Doesn't taste half bad, either."

Yu took the bottle, swirled it, then took a swig. "Hmm. Not bad."

They drank while searching the office for food. A stale bag of pretzels and a few chocolate bars made for a late dinner. It wasn't until later and they were drunk when Kaito started scratching his arm. Even then Yu could see how infected the wound looked.

"Hey," Yu pointed at his arm, "I think we should dig up some antibiotics for that. That looks deep. You'll be lucky if you don't need stitches."

"Way ahead of you." Kaito dug into his pocket and withdrew a plastic baggie filled with pills. He shook the contents. "This should do the trick." He also had some gauze, some medical tape, and some sort of cream.

After a while, they both quieted, sitting beside one another, staring up at the sky. It was Kaito who broke the silence.

"Do you think there's more of those things?"

Yu looked at him. "I'm not sure."

"Well, whatever it was, that thing looked like someone had beaten it with an ugly stick." He scratched his arm. "Damn thing scratched me up bad while we were wrestling, before I could get the sword drawn."

"It was probably just some deformed animal, a mutation or such."

"It didn't look like any animal I've ever seen."

"Whatever it was, it's gone now." Yu looked around. "Guess that's why everyone left."

"Well, we need to get ahead of this, got it?"

Yu nodded.

"Best to find some others and stick with them." Kaito stood. "For now, though, I'm hitting the hay."

And that's how it went the following day, a long day of travel, finding some place to stay the night, and the two brothers foraging for the best makeshift dinner they could find. Throughout their travels, Kaito continued to itch his arm and complain about the mounting pain, even once they stopped for the night. And while Yu stayed up late, Kaito went to bed, leaving Yu to himself in the dark, where he soon nodded off.

Yu woke in a ratty folding chair, slumped down in the seat so far that when he got up, the chair toppled over behind him, startling him. Yawning, he made his way through the house they were staying at, a small ranch home with the door left open, the owner's evidently in such a hurry to leave they didn't care. And that was good because they'd left behind some cans of soup and other food.

In the kitchen, Yu prepared a bowl of cereal, using water instead of milk. He walked with the bowl in hand, scooping spoonful after spoonful into his mouth as he made his way down the hall to the room his brother had claimed.

He knocked on the door. "Hey, you ready to get going?"

No answer.

"Dang it, Kaito. It's too—" Yu threw open the door. "Hey? Kaito?"

If Kaito wasn't here, where was he? Had he gone ahead on his own? That seemed doubtful, especially given the fact he'd left Grandfather's sword behind on the dresser. Something else wasn't right, either, a thing he hadn't noticed at first glance but now saw well enough. A large conical shaped object sat in one corner, just to the right of the nightstand, nearly hidden from view. The closer he got, the more he could define it, but for the life of him, he couldn't decide what it was. His best guess was a hornet's nest. Then again, it looked almost egg-like, but he knew of no creature that birthed anything like that. It had to be a hornet's nest.

Yu decided it was best to leave it alone, whatever it was. And he was certain Kaito would have felt the same way, likely the reason he'd wandered off elsewhere. Yu shut the door behind him and continued searching the house for his brother. But the longer he searched, the more he came up empty.

"Bastard left me," Yu said.

For whatever reason, Kaito had left. Maybe he'd be back, hopefully soon because Yu didn't want to stay here long. If they wanted to stay ahead of this, they needed to get on the road soon. Even now, Yu could hear war machines in the distance, moving in that clinkety-clunkety way. The bombing had stopped, which was good, but the fact he could hear so many vehicles in the distance didn't bode well for them. Plus, they had to steer clear of any military or they'd risk being shipped back. They wouldn't stand a chance if they ran into anyone official.

Yu spent much of the day sitting around, waiting. He tried to stay busy, but it wasn't long before he was itching to go after his brother. Only problem was, he did not know where he might have gone. He was certain it must have been important though, perhaps he'd found their contact and was finishing up business. Once they settled that, they could go wherever they pleased, so that made sense. Maybe Kaito heard the trucks and knew there was little chance of avoiding the military personnel, so he devised a plan to get their paperwork in order before that occurred. That would have been the smart thing to do, and Kaito was slightly smarter than Yu, though he'd never admit that to his brother face to face.

So, Yu just waited, and when it felt like Kaito was gone too long, he waited longer. When night came, he scrounged up a meal and kept waiting. It neared midnight and although he worried, he stayed put, waiting for his brother to return. But Kaito never made it back, because his brother never left. Yu didn't discover that until the following morning.

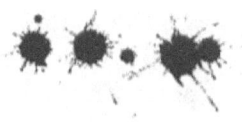

When Kaito didn't return the following day, Yu started to get worried. He checked the room again, and that's when he found it. The cocoon—for now he could see that was what it was—had hatched. Whatever came out of it he found nowhere, but now he worried whatever this thing was that hatched out of that cocoon might have hurt Kaito. Because of that, Yu took up his grandfather's sword and set out to find whatever had hatched in that room.

He kept the scabbard strapped to his back but had the sword drawn in case he ran into trouble. It was late in the afternoon, and the sky was just starting to bruise over when he heard something in a nearby house. Without hesitation, Yu went to investigate. Standing out front of the house, he elbowed the door which had been slightly ajar when he got there. The door creaked open, and Yu stepped inside.

To his left sat a sofa and a couple comfy chairs in a rather ordinary living room. In the distance was the kitchen, an old American seventies-looking décor. Tupperware containers and other empty food receptacles lay scattered across the floor.

He made his way down the hall, toward the bedrooms.

On the way, he passed a bathroom. Nothing caught his eye, save for the torn shower curtain that hung from a couple curtain rings. The bathroom had that same dated look, pink wall tiles with yellow floor tiles, terrible colors to match, in Yu's opinion. The first bedroom appeared plain, just a bed and a nightstand and not much else. The other bedroom door was closed though, which concerned Yu as he approached and stood in front of the door listening.

Bam!

Something had struck the door, and while Yu didn't jump back, he nearly choked on his own saliva. He steadied the sword and placed a hand on the doorknob. Only then did he notice the dirt.

A trail of dirt ran down the hallway, brush and limb and other debris scattered along the way. Why he hadn't noticed it before was beyond him, but now he saw it well. Something had been dragging earthly debris into the house and apparently into this room. For what purpose, he didn't know.

Yu opened the door.

What he saw made his eyes widen. A creature—the kind from nightmares—stood against the far wall, using mud and sticks and limbs it had gathered in its arms to form a nest. It wasn't a large nest, but it was big enough for the three cocoons sitting in the middle. That moment came and went, as the creature's wings shot out at its sides, making an intimidating appearance. It planned to attack Yu, and he didn't know what to do. He'd seen nothing of this magnitude.

In Yu's mind, he saw something else happen right then. His brother Kaito came running in to save the day, seizing their grandfather's sword, and getting right to work. In Yu's thoughts, Kaito sliced that monster down to size in seconds. In reality, Kaito never showed up, and Yu just stood there, sword in hand, as the creature attacked.

A rush of air shook Yu out of his statuesque pose, and the sword came to life. With little forethought, the sword cut through the air fast as lightning. A second later, a thump drew Yu's attention to the floor where he saw the arm.

The creature backed away.

Yu moved in, and before the creature could escape, he had severed one of its wings. A crash of glass and a trail of blood followed the creature's progress as it plummeted through the window. Yu saw it staggering across the lawn and hurried through the window after it. The creature got maybe twelve yards before Yu caught up to it. Without hesitation, he went to work. In a matter of seconds, he'd dissected the creature, turning it into a quadriplegic. Even then it tried to get away and seeing it struggle, a terrifying thought occurred to Yu for the first.

What if this is Kaito?

No, that wasn't possible. Was it?

Could these creatures—now that he had seen one—be humans that had transformed? He would expect this much from the big screen, but not in real life. It couldn't be possible. But seeing it now, that tattoo on the creature's severed arm, it was hard to deny.

The creature stared up at him with a single hurt-filled eye. That eye was larger than it should be, but Yu saw it all the same. And he hadn't hesitated once in taking his brother's arms and legs and...wings?

"Do. It," Kaito said, struggling to speak at all. The overwhelming amount of blood loss implied he would bleed out before this was over, anyway. "Help. Me."

If Kaito was still in there, he'd just willed the creature to speak for him. And if Yu fully believed this was his brother, he had to obey his wishes. He stood over his brother, not seeing him for who he once was but for what he had become, and with one swipe, he took his brother's head.

The moment came and went, but the sorrow that filled Yu overwhelmed him. He collapsed to the ground, weeping, watching his brother's alien form deteriorate. And Yu wept for a long time afterward, even after the shadows appeared. That was when he realized they'd surrounded him, three other creatures just like his brother.

Yu reached for the sword, and the creatures moved in. He was up and on his feet, sword drawn back, before they came within range. Yu made quick work of them, leaving them in much the same state as his brother. If need be, he would stay here all day fighting them off like this if that meant he could end them. Doing that might make him feel better about what he had done. But he couldn't stay, no matter how badly he wanted to. Having to spend any more time here staring at his deceased brother would crush him. But he couldn't leave his brother's handiwork intact.

Yu made his way back to the house and to the bedroom where he once more confronted the nest. He could have just burned the house, and he certainly felt like doing so, but he didn't want to draw any attention to himself. He needed to stay clear of the military and lighting a house on fire wouldn't exactly achieve that goal. Instead, he used the sword to dissect the cocoons, paying close attention to their construction and what was inside. With care, he cut a line through the first layer of one cocoon, and the husk fell away, leaving behind a brownish-gray layer. That, too, Yu cut away with care, revealing a more translucent shell, but Yu couldn't make sense of what he was seeing inside. He saw fingers surrounded by some gelatinous goo, that much he was certain about. And they were human fingers, but not everything he saw appeared human. He couldn't tell what those parts were, not yet. So, he made his final cut and watched as the blood and viscera and limbs fell to the ground in a pile of warm steaming liquid.

What the fuck?

And that was the question of the day. What he saw was human, not entirely but mostly. At least it used to be human. Now, what remained of the pile of body parts—which all appeared to belong to the same human judging by their size and pigmentation—was some malformed...*thing*. Not a human being or even a creature but something in-between those two entities. This was an abomination.

The next cocoon revealed much the same, but the third wasn't human at all. Its contents were the same, but these parts weren't human by any means. They'd put one of their own in the cocoon, evidence that what they were hatching from these cocoons didn't need to be alive—not fully, at least—and didn't even have to be human. They could rebuild them, bring them back to life, and that meant—

Kaito!

Yu ran outside and got there just in time to see a creature gathering the pieces.

"Put him down!" Yu said.

The creature ignored him. It flapped its menacing wings, but at no cost would it drop those body parts. Realizing this,

Yu charged, sword raised, ready to strike. The creature flapped its wings, preparing to take flight. By the time Yu reached it, the creature was three yards off the ground, its arms filled with alien body parts. Yu stepped on the torso of one of the fallen corpses that was being left behind and leaped into the sky. Midair, he swung the blade wildly, shredding the creature's wings badly enough that it fell back to earth.

There, Yu cut it down to size as he had the others...his brother. When he finished, he dragged the bodies from inside the house out and made a pile. Seeing this made his heart wretch, as he poured lighter fluid all over them and lit the mound. Only when they were burning, those that were still alive, crying out in pain, did the weight of what he was doing fall upon him.

I killed him.

And that was true. He had killed his brother. Now he had nothing left in this world. He only hoped to find his way home. But how could he ever explain this to his parents? Not only would they not believe him, even if they did, they would never understand why he had taken such action. Yu didn't fully understand it himself. He'd taken an oath to protect his brother. And Kaito was the strong one, not Yu. How was Yu supposed to get by on his own? What was he supposed to do now?

Over the next few weeks, Yu made his way across the eastern United States. Sadly, everywhere he went, it was always the same. To date, he had killed and burned more creatures than he could ever count. He had seen few humans and when he did, he avoided all contact. All he wanted was for everyone to leave him alone.

Then, one day while walking through a city, he saw someone waving him down. As he neared the man, Yu thought he looked friendly enough. Strangely, even though this man was white, he reminded Yu of his brother. It was something about the way the man carried himself, like a born leader. And perhaps that was why Yu stopped to talk to him, a man that went by the name Marty.

When Marty asked about the sword, Yu had thought little of it. At first, the questions were easy, the sort one asks when they're interested in something. Marty had taken an interest in the sword. But, in time, those questions became personal, and as they did, the moments soured, until one day the memories of what Yu had done to his brother became too much. That day, Yu left the sword behind and ventured west on his own, determined to find somewhere he could be alone, to heal, on his own.

Maybe, if he could do that, someday he could return.

About the Author

Kenneth W. Cain is an author of horror and dark fiction, and a Splatterpunk Award nominated freelance editor and graphic designer. To date, he has had over one hundred short stories and thirteen novels/novellas, as well as a handful each of nonfiction pieces, books for children, and poems released by many publishers, such as Crystal Lake Publishing and JournalStone. He has also edited seven anthologies. Cain lives in Chester County PA with his family, and suffers from chronic pain. As such, he likes to keep busy and spends more time working than socializing. His full publishing history is available on his website at kennethwcain.com.

As an Active member of the Horror Writers Association, he is chair for the membership committee, heads the Pennsylvania chapter, and was given the 2017 Silver Hammer Award for his service. Currently, Cain helps several publishers with their editing, formatting, book cover, and graphic design needs. Cain resides in Chester County, Pennsylvania with his wife and two children.

At an early age Cain heard a reading of the Baba Yaga folklore and fell in love with dark fiction and horror. That love was nurtured during his formative years in the suburbs of Chicago, listening to his grandfather spin far-fetched tales beside the glow of a barrel fire. Shows like *The Twilight Zone*, *The Outer Limits*, *Alfred Hitchcock Presents*, and *One Step Beyond* furthered his wonder of the unknown, the unexplainable, and he's been writing ever since. In his free time, when he isn't reading or writing, he enjoys the outdoors, fine art, and sports.

Curious about other Crossroad Press books?
Stop by our site:
http://store.crossroadpress.com
We offer quality writing
in digital, audio, and print formats.

www.ingramcontent.com/pod-product-compliance
Lightning Source LLC
Chambersburg PA
CBHW031133210626
46816CB00014B/705